ACCLAIM

"The complexity of *And Then There Were None* meets a rousing game of *Clue* in this twisty country house mystery!"
—ALYSSA MAXWELL, author of The Gilded Newport Mysteries

"With its cast of intriguing characters, clever plot, and witty repartee, Murder at Mistlethwaite Manor is a delightful foray into Victorian England that's perfect for fans of cozy mysteries and historical fiction."
—IRINA SHAPIRO, bestselling author of the Redmond and Haze Mysteries

"*Murder at Mistlethwaite Manor* is a classic 'whodunit' story that had me rapidly turning pages to puzzle out what happened next. Skelly crafts a fast-paced tale reminiscent of *Clue*, with plenty of suspects and ever-lurking danger afoot. The story also dishes up a healthy portion of delicious romantic drama, witty dialogue, and beautiful descriptions. This book is sure to delight mystery readers everywhere, especially those who like a little romance sprinkled on top."

—ASHLEY BUSTAMANTE, bestselling author of The Color Theory trilogy

"A page-turning Christmas read perfect for historical mystery lovers, *Murder at Mistlethwaite Manor* provides a jaunty and delightful whodunnit frolic through the most wonderful time of the year, Gilded-Age style!"

—CHELSEA BOBULSKI, author of the All I Want for Christmas series

"A novella for the Agatha Christie fan in you looking through the next literary door for another dead body, *Murder at Mistlethwaite Manor* is a tale of intrigue written with Skelly's trademark swoon, heart-pounding moments, and a lovely dash of wit. As the mystery unravels, you'll be simultaneously wishing you could join the gathering at Mistlethwaite Manor—a delightfully gothic location plucked straight from the English moors and likely your favourite books—while also thanking your lucky stars that you missed this particular invitation, because though the setting is marvelous and the romance is lovely, there's scandal and danger afoot!"

—BRITTANY EDEN, award-winning author of *Wishes* and *Hearts*

"With mischief and mayhem around every corner, *Murder at Mistlethwaite Manor* is difficult to put down! Skelly adds just enough intrigue to each character to keep the reader guessing as to who the murderer really is. This "whodunnit" story is an excellent beginning to hopefully more books by AJ Skelly in this genre."

—V. ROMAS BURTON, award-winning author of the Heartmaker trilogy and Legacy Chapters

"*Murder at Mistlethwaite Manor* is a deliciously fast-paced murder mystery reminiscent of the movie Clue that will keep you spellbound until the very end! Skelly paints an enchanting visual with a cast of characters that are wildly addictive. Fiercely romantic with hilarious banter, this tale will keep you guessing until the very last page. Imaginative and delightful, this is easily my favorite book of 2024."

—LAURA L. ZIMMERMAN, award-winning author of *Keen*

"5 stars to AJ Skelly's *Murder at Mistlethwaite Manor*. A gripping historical mystery that will keep you guessing until the very end! Perfect for fans of Agatha Christie and The Gilded Age—but be warned. You won't be able to put this one down!"

—MERRIE DESTEFANO, USA Today bestselling author of *Shade*, *Lost Girls*, and *Empire of Ruin*

"Delightfully mysterious and perfectly plotted. *Murder at Mistlethwaite Manor* offers a closed circle tale perfect for fans of

Agatha Christie but with a Victorian twist and just the right touch of romance. You'll feel the bite of the winter chill while you fight to stay a step ahead of a killer bent on deception and death."

—E. A. HENDRYX, author of the Xerus Galaxy Saga

Murder at MISTLETHWAITE MANOR

Murder at
MISTLETHWAITE MANOR

Quill & Flame
PUBLISHING HOUSE

AJ SKELLY

Quill & Flame

Murder at Mistlethwaite Manor

Copyright ©2024 by AJ Skelly

Published by Quill & Flame Publishing House, an imprint of Book Bash Media, LLC.

www.quillandflame.com

Cover design by EAHCreative

For Amanda

Thank you for your constant encouragement
while I wrote this story.

It might not have happened without you.

Mr. Clarance Campbell

Andrew Harrigan
Lord Stanford

Raymond Stockard
Lord Villiers

Percival Crofton
Lord Fairfax

Mr. William Angus

Miss Emma Grace
Lady Hastings

Mrs. Margaret Wentworth

Mrs. Rose Weatherton
Lady Algernon

Mrs. Francis Banks
Lady Fulbright

Mr. Bert Humphrey
Lord Asquith

OTHER BOOKS BY AJ SKELLY

The Wolves of Rock Falls

First Shift

Rogue Shift

Sworn Shift

Dark Shift

Pack Shift

The Wolves of Arcadia Bay

Lost Shift

Magik Prep Academy

Of Flame & Frost

Making Magik

CHAPTER ONE

The envelope was heavy in my trembling hand. Detaching the golden wax seal, my fingers shook as I slid one beneath the flap.

"Ouch!" My finger came away red, sliced by the thick paper. One drop of blood fell onto the pristine missive.

"Oh, I've ruined it," I muttered, wiping blood off my hand with a silken handkerchief.

I should have taken the omen for what it was and steered clear. But unwitting as I was, what with the now-broken wax seal promising all the thrill of the unknown, I reverently opened the envelope and pulled out the invitation within as if it were made of diamonds. The swirling calligraphy of Mistlethwaite's master captured my imagination. I inhaled sharply at my name at the top of the letter.

Lady Hastings,

You are cordially invited to attend a most auspicious holiday gathering at Mistlethwaite Manor. Chaperones will be provided. Bring only your brightest holiday garments. Nothing more. A Ten Thousand Pound prize to the guest who can solve the puzzle presented at the party.

Yours truly,

The Master of Mistlethwaite

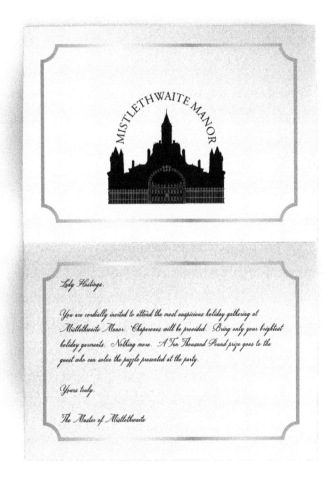

Lady Hastings,

You are cordially invited to attend the most auspicious holiday gathering at Mistlethwaite Manor. Chaperones will be provided. Bring only your brightest holiday garments. Nothing more. A Ten Thousand Pound prize goes to the guest who can solve the puzzle presented at the party.

Yours truly,

The Master of Mistlethwaite

I held my breath and stared at the weighty card as I clutched it in my trembling hands.

Mistlethwaite Manor.

One of the most picturesque manors on the Eastern coast of Britain. One accessible by invitation only. For the past three Christmases, only ten missives had been sent out each season among the peers—the very top of society, and each year, there had been some enormous prize to be won. It occupied the gossips for months on end. *Everyone* wanted to be invited to a Christmas Puzzle Party at Mistlethwaite. One of the best kept secrets among the ton, not even the host or hostess's identity was confirmed. Despite the popularity of these parties for the past holiday seasons, no one had divulged the secrets surrounding Mistlethwaite Manor.

I never dreamed I'd warrant such a solicitation. Though I was aristocracy through and through, chances were remote that from among the ton I might receive one of the coveted invitations. I was positively thrilled to my fingertips to find myself a recipient.

My stunned bliss was surpassed only by my mother's unbridled joy, albeit laced with anxiety. The sight of blood didn't help; I hid the envelope and soiled handkerchief behind my back.

"Emma Grace, there is not time for Worth to draw you up a new gown," fretted my mother. I smiled, running my finger along the smooth edge of the crisply folded invitation. Gilt edges winked at me as the weak winter sunlight filtered through the windows of my bedroom.

"Who do you think he is?" I asked, the words a reverent hush upon my lips.

"Who do I think…what are you saying, my dear girl?" Mother stopped her pacing in front of my bursting armoire to look at me, one slender dark brow raised in question.

"The Master of Mistlethwaite. No one knows his true identity." My imagination ran wild.

"All the more reason to impress. I've heard rumors it is Prince Edward himself." Mother gave me a knowing look and smiled deep enough that lines bracketed her mouth.

My heart fluttered. "Do you really think it's him?"

"I wish I knew. That sort of information is worth its weight in gold, as the saying goes." Her smile fell as she pursed her lips, perusing my person. "I do worry that you won't have anyone to do up your hair. You're sure the invite instructs you not to bring even a lady's maid?"

I handed her the thick, cream-colored card. She tucked her bottom lip into her mouth, a habit she only indulged in private. She tsked. "Seems a bit uncharitable not to let a lady bring her full entourage."

I laughed. "Mother, it's only for a long weekend. Surely, I can manage my own tresses and dresses for that amount of time."

Mother's eyes brimmed with unshed tears of pride and happiness. "I'm delighted for you, Emma Grace. Your father is, too, despite his grousing. You'll do us all proud, I'm certain. Perhaps this invitation will make you all the more desirable to young Lord Fairfax." She sniffed.

Percival Crofton, Lord Fairfax. His ancestral title. Heat rushed to my cheeks. Percy who had chosen me when scandal would have buried me. Percy, who had treasured my broken heart. Percy, who had saved me—both from society and from myself. Percy, on whom all my hopes currently rested. Percy, who was the safe choice that would bring security to my future and to my family. Percy, who I would choose to love despite what my heart whispered. "I would not object to this turn of events."

Mother tittered. "I'd say not. Don't you worry, my girl. Society has surely forgotten what misfortune befell you two years ago. It is time to move on with your life, and I cannot think of anyone more suited to move on with than the young Lord Fairfax."

A shiver of darkness whispered through me. The *misfortune* my mother spoke of still pressed heavily against my chest. Betrayal and shame were not easily overcome in my society, and at times, my heart still ached with the memories. But it was time. Most assuredly. My twentieth birthday was drawing near and if Percy Crofton didn't take me to wife, I'd find myself an old maid whose prospects were as shriveled as aged raisins.

CHAPTER TWO

A puff of breath plumed in front of my face and snow dusted the tops of my shoes as the footman handed me down from the black carriage, spruced with sprigs of vibrant holly.

The front of Mistlethwaite Manor was astounding, both in sheer size as well as in opulence. Pale gray stone rose into the sky, turrets kissing the setting sun as towers and crenelations battled for dominance. It stretched so far in either direction I had to turn my head to see all the vast expanse.

"Might I accompany you indoors, Lady Hastings?" my carriage man asked.

"Of course." I stopped my wool gathering and let the footman take my elbow lest I slip on the slick sheet of ice that lay beneath the snow. In truth, the journey to the manor had been rather perilous.

Had the prestige and possible outcome not been so propitious, I wouldn't have dared to come at all in such ghastly weather.

As if to concur with my thoughts, a fierce wind whipped down from the eves, thrashing my scarf tight against my throat like a hangman's noose. Tugging at it and clamping a hand onto my precariously pinned hat, we struggled to the door.

"Lady Hastings, welcome to Mistlethwaite Manor," said a middle-aged man clothed resplendently in black with a festive red bow tie. "Please see to the lady's luggage, then you may depart." The man I presumed was the butler addressed my footman.

It was a little disconcerting to summarily have one's staff dismissed, but the missive from the Master of Mistlethwaite *had* stressed that only the invited were welcome. It was part of the grand adventure and smacked in the gentlest way possible of the acceptable sort of daring behavior not normally allowed young, unwed, well-bred English girls. Such as myself.

"If my lady will follow me." The butler gave a little head nod, and we proceeded up a truly impressive staircase and down a chilly corridor dazzled with facets of light bouncing from the lit gas lamps reflecting off the stained-glass windows. The wind howled against the stone walls and the sound echoed like the distant shriek of a banshee down the long, decorated hallway.

Even festooned for the Christmas season with evergreen, holly berries, and smelling sweetly of spiced oranges, said cheer couldn't suppress the eeriness that permeated the air. A little shiver worked up my spine at the ghostly screeching of the wind. As we ascended a set of steps and entered an antechamber, a maid appeared from a hidden door in the paneling. Clever, to disguise servant's doors within the wainscoting. In our estate, servants had to use the back stairs. Moving through the walls was like pure magic.

"I'll take your wraps, my lady." She dipped a quick curtsy and took my heavy wool cape, stole, and scarf. Discreetly fluffing the wine-colored puffed sleeves at my shoulders, I hoped I wasn't too rumpled should I run into anyone important before having the chance to freshen up. Excitement thrummed in my belly as I thought about the possibilities of who else might have been invited.

The butler indicated the maid. "My wife, Mrs. Leonard, will show you to your quarters where tea will be served. You may freshen yourself and change for dinner. Your presence is requested at half past six in the drawing room. Do not be late, or you may be disqualified from the game and the prize."

Before I could utter even a word of response, the butler—Mr. Leonard—nodded and disappeared down the hallway.

"If you'll follow me, my lady." The same maid, skin pale and hair nearly white blonde under her tidy white cap, bobbed a curtsy and indicated I should follow her down another chilly hallway. Thick, vibrant carpets muffed our steps as I trailed the woman, trying not to ogle outright at the vast displays of wealth lining the walls. Paintings, statuary, tables inlaid with mother of pearl and studded with semi-precious stones. Tapestries likely worth more than a king's ransom covered huge swaths of the stone.

We traipsed up three flights of curving stairs to yet another ornate hallway, this one dark with alternating paneled wood and red and gold damask cloth.

"Your chambers, my lady. All the guest chambers are here on the third floor. Women to the right side of the hallway, men to the left. Do you require anything else momentarily? Your luggage should all be present and accounted for."

I stepped inside the room and delighted in the dazzling array of lush greens and soft pinks, completed by a sparkling chandelier hanging from the middle of the room. Glass orbs dangled from its gilt arms, bending and refracting the light into a thousand rainbows across the walls and into the shadowed corners of the room. My trunk and suitcase were stacked neatly beside a cherry wood vanity, which was set with a silver comb, brush, and mirror. Another card with my name on it lay on its marble surface next to a steaming tea tray.

Excitement hummed beneath my skin, and suddenly I couldn't wait to be alone to tear into this newest missive from my most elusive host.

I would avoid bloody hands this time.

"That will be all, thank you," I demurred.

Once the door was shut, I abandoned all decorum, hiking my skirts above my ankles and racing to snatch the missive.

Tearing the envelope open like a savage, I slowed and reverently took out the folded card.

Lady Hastings,

Welcome to Mistlethwaite Manor. I trust your stay here will be most memorable. Please wear your finest holiday frock to dinner tonight. The games will begin promptly at half past six. Bring all your wit and charm and come prepared.

Yours truly,

The Master of Mistlethwaite

Lady Hastings,

Welcome to Mistlethwaite Manor. I trust your stay here will be most memorable. Please wear your finest holiday frock to dinner tonight. The games will begin promptly at half past six. Bring with you all your wit, charm, and come prepared.

Yours truly,

The Master of Mistlethwaite

Come prepared?

Prepared for what?

I tapped the letter against my bottom lip then caught my reflection in the mirror.

"Oh, good gracious!" Muttering dropped unceremoniously from my lips as I took in my ghastly windblown hair. Thank heavens none but the staff had happened upon me in such a state. The clock in the corner of the room chimed. Five o'clock. I had scarcely an hour before I needed to make my descent into the dining room. I hoped I could find my way there in plenty of time. Old estates like these were a positive labyrinth of corridors and rooms. I glanced at the clock again, the world a swirl of white through the window beyond it. Perhaps I'd better plan on a few extra moments just to be safe.

CHAPTER THREE

C lothed in a forest green silk Worth creation trimmed in costly lace, I was clad for a successful entrance. I added a miniature gilded pinecone pinned at my throat, and little red dangles in my lobes. Most importantly, I'd ensured my hair was as artfully arranged as I could manage. I was presentable.

From the front.

I sighed.

Truly, I needed a lady's maid to properly tame my wild chocolate-colored curls. The front of my Gibson Girl bun was smoothed save only the naturally curling tendrils near my face. I shoved one more pin in unceremoniously to the back of the knot, daring my unruly hair to even think of falling this evening.

I blinked into the mirror, checking that my hazel eyes sparkled in the lamp light. Pinching my cheeks and biting down on my lips to make sure they were appropriately rosy, I deemed myself acceptable.

Quite satisfactory, if I was being completely honest and not practicing modesty as a young woman should. And if one ignored the back of my hair. I gave myself a saucy wink in the mirror, then blushed, knowing I'd never have the gall to do such a brazen thing. What would Percy Crofton think of me if I did? Fanning myself lest my blush ruin my porcelain complexion, I drew a black silk shawl over my shoulders. Festive as things were, and cheery as the fires in the hearths might be, it was still frigid in the long halls, and it was time for me to find my way to the drawing room.

It wouldn't do to be late. Not at all. I was curious as to the other invited guests as well. Anticipation hummed along my arms.

The hallways were chilled, and more than a little ominous, causing me to draw my shawl a bit closer. The gas lighting was bright but cast long, dark shadows across the walls. Though I saw no other staff or invitees, I could hear occasional sounds that went beyond the creaking of the old mansion. People, and living ones, I assured myself. Though I warranted parts of the manor dated back to the time of William the Conqueror.

I was good at directions—better than most girls of my acquaintance—and it didn't take long to find the corridor where Mr. Leonard had deposited me with his wife. I assumed finding the drawing room was part of the first puzzle, since I hadn't been given directions, and honestly, had been too excited by the cream envelope awaiting me on the dressing table to think to ask instructions of Mrs. Leonard.

Pushing open a heavy wooden door decorated in a stunning bas-relief of animals and mythological creatures, a blood red carpet runner led directly into a great hall. The enormous space was breathtaking. I would have liked to study the intricacies for hours on end. Fearing tardiness should I dally, and wanting to spy out the other guests, I did my best to ignore the gilded trappings and the medieval style paintings adorning both ceiling and walls. Marble statuary looked on as I quickened my pace through the magnificent ballroom toward the doors leading off it. Likely, one of those was the sought-after drawing room. My low-heeled slippers made soft clicks against the white and black marble floor, and I was suddenly overcome with a desire to dance across it, held in the arms of my beau.

Percy Crofton would eat his tongue when I told him of my weekend at Mistlethwaite Manor! I hoped Mother was correct and that my invitation to Mistlethwaite would further raise my estimation in Percy's eyes.

Poking my head into the first door on the far side of the great hall, I was met with cold blackness. Not the room I required.

Creaking open another door, I was rewarded with a roaring fire in the grate, lamps lit, and a Christmas tree decked in glittering ornaments, flickering candles, and ropes of red satin cord. I wasn't sure I'd ever seen anything so festive.

Glancing around, it appeared I was early. I breathed a little sigh of relief. I'd much rather be early than late, even if some insisted being fashionably late was the thing. I preferred to arrive early and watch everyone else—and in some cases, let myself be seen upon their entrance. I let my eyes wander, briefly noting nooks and crannies—little alcoves hidden in lush draperies and festooned with holiday ornamentation. Mistletoe and holly sprigs, it seemed. A piece of furniture creaked, and my head whipped around, my gaze landing on the very last person I expected to see.

Andrew Harrigan.

My erstwhile fiancé, former friend, first love, and now much publicly made pauper. Surprise tightened my throat even as my heart cracked.

Andrew's eyes widened. "Emma Grace," he whispered then cleared his throat. "I mean, Lady Hastings." He stuttered a half bow, as if unsure of his actions. In all the time I'd known him, even when his family lost their fortune, Andrew had never been less than confident in himself. Until he stood before me now, looking lost and uncertain.

Emotions threatened to erupt. I glanced around, assuring myself that there were no prying eyes before grabbing his sleeve and dragging him with me into an alcove, shadowed by thick red velvet draperies and copious Christmas garland. Snow gusted against the windowpane, the chill wind making its way in through the cracks around the wavy glass. I shivered. "Andrew, what are you doing here?" My whispered words sounded harsh as they scraped over the ball of emotion fisted in my throat.

My heart was not over Andrew Harrigan—though Percy Crofton's kind attentions had helped ease the pain of my longing—and part of me feared the Harrigan family had sunk low enough that Andrew was here as hired help. Furious as I still was with my former fiancé, I wasn't sure I could bear it for him if that were the case.

His gaze softened as he took me in. He swallowed, his expression going carefully neutral. "I got an invitation, and since the prize for solving the master's puzzle would more than solve my family's financial burdens, I could hardly decline." The words were stiff. He ran a hand through his caramel-colored hair, and my mouth dried.

"I'm sorry. I didn't mean for that to...sound insulting." The words died off.

He gave me a brittle smile.

Andrew glanced down at my hand, still clenched in the fabric of his evening coat, and I snatched it back. I fidgeted my fingers in front of me, clasping them and unclasping them only to grab hold of my skirt and let it go.

"I am all but engaged to Percy Crofton," I blurted, wincing at how callous the words sounded out of my mouth.

His face smoothed into an unreadable mask. "I heard. Felicitations." Did the words strangle themselves from his throat? Perhaps he needed a sip of punch.

"Thank you." I swallowed. Perhaps *I* needed that glass of punch. Old anger toward Andrew simmered like live coals beneath my skin. Wounds I thought were healing suddenly cracked open, oozing and raw. "Please excuse me." I legged a hasty retreat from the alcove, shoving down the ache of rejection that surfaced upon coming face to face with Andrew Harrigan again.

Resentment that he'd called off our engagement. Anger that he'd left me. Pain that he'd broken my heart. And all because of fortunes. Status.

I took a shuddering breath. *It didn't matter*, I told myself. I had Percy now. And society said he was a far better catch than *Mr. Harrigan* ever had been—even before his family had lost all their money. I must marry Percy to ensure my own security and connections for my family. And Andr—Mr. Harrigan did not want me. I swallowed.

Truthfully, I expected Percy's proposal soon. He'd not lavish me with such attention as he had if he had no plans for a future that included me. I was fairly certain my invitation to the holiday festivities at Mistlethwaite would be the final solidification in his mind. The glow that often accompanied such thoughts was smothered by the shock of finding Mr. Harrigan here. If Andrew did anything to upset my chances, he'd rue the day he ever laid eyes on me. He'd broken my heart once; I would not allow him to break it a second time.

Refusing to let such tempestuous thoughts show on my face, I blew out a hot breath, held my head high, straightened my carriage and pinched my cheeks, hoping the rest of my face wasn't all mottled. Putting on a smooth exterior, I determined to enjoy myself and do my family name proud.

Blessedly, the door opened again, and a tall gentleman near my own age slinked through the doorway. He was handsome in a laid back, not quite gentry sort of way.

"Ah, I see I'm not the first to arrive," he said pleasantly, a slight Scottish lilt to his words. His dark eyes cast about, taking in his surroundings. He whistled appreciatively.

"I'm Andrew Harrigan." Andr—Mr. Harrigan moved toward the new man, extending his hand. Interesting that he did not use his ancestral title. He might be penniless, but he was still Lord Stanford.

"Clarence Campbell." The men shook and Clarence turned to me. "Miss, pleasure to make your acquaintance." He tipped his head.

I cleared my throat. "Lady. Lady Emma Grace Hastings."

"Begging your pardon then." Was that mockery shining in his eyes? Another twist of uncertainty slithered into my belly.

"What is this? Am I missing a party?" Another young man entered, his carefully pomaded hair shining against the gas lights. "Bert Humphrey, newly made Lord Asquith. Still not used to the title!" He laughed heartily at his own amusement. He carried himself with such assurance that no one could be in question that he'd been raised with privilege. His gaze met mine and quickly traveled my person. "It is *nice* to meet you."

I tried not to squirm under his clear perusal. Mr. Harrigan cleared his throat and took a step nearer me.

"Indeed, it is," said a familiar voice from behind. Relief flooded enough to weaken my bones as I whirled to find none other than

Percy Crofton outlined in the doorway. His broad shoulders and trim waist cast impressive shadows into the hallway behind him. My belly did a little flip.

Percy smiled warmly at me before glaring at the young newcomer. The juvenile Lord Asquith shrugged and smiled as if he hadn't a care in the world. Percy took in the rest of the room, eyes growing round, showing whites all around his blue irises, as his gaze fell on Andrew Harrigan. The three of us were in all the same social circles—or we had been before the Harrigans fell into ruin. Now all Andrew's family held was an empty title, devoid of anything behind it. And the stinging residue of rumors from our broken engagement.

"Lord Fairfax." Andrew's deep voice cut through the awkward silence that had descended.

"*Mr.* Harrigan," Percy said stiffly, using Andrew's familiar name, rather than his empty title. Andrew's jaw ticked. Percy turned his attention to me, irritation melting as his smile stretched across his face. "And Lady Hastings. It is certainly a pleasure to find you here."

"Indeed. I was most pleased to be invited." Conflicting emotions churned in my gut as Percy crossed the room, seized my hand, and gently kissed the back of it—a gesture he'd done, and I'd appreciated, many times before. I pasted a smile on my lips but couldn't help when my eyes flitted to Andrew, his face a stony mask of indifference.

I should not care what he thought.

I absolutely should not.

But I found, to my utmost consternation, that I did. I was uncomfortable with Percy's attentions in front of Andrew. But why on earth should I be? *Andrew* left *me.* He didn't want me. Percy did. I loved Percy. I was going to marry the man, as soon as he asked me. It would be a glorious wedding and we'd be one of the best matched couples in all of Britain.

I was saved from further disgruntling thoughts by the arrival of two other women. Both likely in their late thirties or early forties, they were attired in the latest fashions. Shantung silk, if I wasn't mistaken, folds of lace, sparkling beads, and at least five ropes of pearls between them.

"What a grand little party we've all come to attend," the shorter said. She was clad in pink silk with black lace flounces.

"Indeed, but where is our host?" The taller woman, her brown hair having the slightest gray streaks at the temples, glanced about the room questioningly. Her expression was haughty, judgmental. I was instantly wary of her.

"I don't believe he's here just yet? Allow me to make introductions." Percy took charge as a gentleman of breeding should.

"I am Lady Algernon," the woman in pink silk said. Ah. She was an interesting woman—or so her reputation said. I'd never before met her, but rumor had it that Rose Algernon—I had forgotten her maiden name—had toured the Continent when she'd been but sixteen, returned home, and promptly married the aged Earl of Balliol, who then died under mysterious circumstances not two months later. She'd been a widow ever since.

"And I am Mrs. Margaret Wentworth." The taller woman smoothed a hand down her silver beaded skirt.

Wentworth? "Begging your pardon, but of the wool manufacturing Wentworths?" I asked. A flash of something akin to pain crossed Mrs. Wentworth's face and I wished I could take the words back.

"The very same," she said with false brightness. I smiled, keeping more words to myself, lest I further injure the woman. She must be the widow of the former Mr. Wentworth, a minor lord—before he hung himself. The scandal was reported all over the country in hushed whispers. Castigating myself for my own disapproving attitude, I wondered how Mrs. Wentworth could afford such an extravagant gown. It was said that Mr. Wentworth's untimely demise was caused due to his financial ruin. I swallowed hard and couldn't help my eyes flitting once more to Andrew—Mr. Harrigan. Poor Mrs. Wentworth. Poor Andr—Mr. Harrigan.

His expression was one of carefully guarded pity and understanding. Clearly, the rumors of her ruin had reached him, too.

"At last, we've found the right room," a jolly, booming voice said from the doorway.

Three more entered. Two of them I already had on acquaintance. Lord Villiers, a tall man with iron gray hair, quite fit for a man passing middle age. Lady Francis Fulbright, whose gaze was already vivid as if she'd had a sip of spirits, faint wrinkles webbing at the corners of her eyes. And lastly, a plain man in a cheap black wool suit. Neat and tidy, but clearly not one of the upper crust.

"William Angus," the man introduced himself plainly, his Scottish brogue more pronounced than Mr. Campbell's.

The clock in the corner chimed the half hour.

"It seems there are ten of us gathered. There are only ten invitations that go out, are there not? We must be the lucky bunch." Bert Humphrey, Lord Asquith, rubbed his hands together. "Who else is dying to know what puzzle we are to solve?"

"It seems we must wait for our tardy host before we can find out," Lady Fulbright said, consulting the grandfather clock that had chimed only moments ago.

"I have a devilishly quick mind, so best look out. I fully intend to solve this year's puzzle," Clarence Campbell said with a slow, smirking smile. He cracked a knuckle, and the sound raked a finger of irritation over my shoulders.

"Has anyone the faintest clue *who* our host is? This mysterious Master of Mistlethwaite? He seems the best kept secret in the whole of England," Lord Villiers said.

"Do you have any guesses as to his identity, my darling?" Percy said quietly next to my ear.

My darling. I shivered, though still felt awkward and self-conscious as Percy took my hand and draped it over the crook of his elbow. I glanced at his face, his blue eyes twinkling, and tried not to draw any comparisons to the pair of rich, brown eyes I felt boring holes into the side of my head.

"I've heard it might be the prince himself," I whispered, unwilling for everyone in the room to hear my opinion.

"I've heard the same. We shall have to wait and be amazed." He smiled at me, as if he was party to some secret delight, and let his thumb trace once over the back of my hand. My shoulders relaxed a fraction, content at Percy's side, though I did wish such a display of affection weren't in front of Andr—Mr. Harrigan.

"You do suppose he's coming, don't you?" Mrs. Wentworth said.

"Perhaps he is a she? Maybe the Master is really a Mistress?" Lord Asquith suggested.

Lord Villiers threw him a dirty look. "Be reasonable. What nonsense."

"I can assure you all, I am no woman, but one hundred percent male of the finest caliber." A tall man stood shadowed in the doorway. He took one step forward and the light from the room illumined his face.

A collective gasp of horror rose from the room.

CHAPTER FOUR

I ce lodged behind my heart and the blood froze in my veins.

Lord Horace Barclay.

Earl. Cheat. Shrewd. Reprehensible. Possibly the most disgusting man with whom I'd ever had the misfortune of introduction. Only two months ago he'd made lascivious verbal advances upon me at a ball. I'd made sure Percy was aware, and he'd kept close to ward off any further unwanted attention.

But instead of glancing at Percy, my gaze arrested on Mr. Harrigan. For it was widely rumored that it was Horace Barclay that had made the ill-fated business transaction with Andrew's father that resulted in the loss of the family's fortunes. Andrew's knuckles were white, his fingernails surely cutting crescents into his palm.

His jaw was locked, his nostrils flared. He said not a word but loathing practically radiated off his broad shoulders.

Beside me, Lady Algernon gasped, a sharp noise that echoed in the sudden stillness of the room.

Percy's eyes were wide as if he were frightened, his face ashen, the muscles of his forearm taut beneath my fingers. Perhaps he, too, was now dreading the weekend, knowing the cad had made advances toward me.

Mrs. Wentworth was either too shocked to hide her displeasure or she did not care if our host saw it plainly.

Clarence Campbell stared at Lord Barclay, appearing for all the world as bored as if he were watching paint dry.

The others in the room showed varying degrees of surprise. My heart sank. I'd so been looking forward to the mysteries of Mistlethwaite, and now all those hopes seemed dashed at the thought of spending so much time in Lord Barclay's association. I'd happily stay close to Percy again to ensure I avoided as much unpleasantness as possible.

How could such a deliciously mysterious holiday intrigue be centered around such a ghastly, disgraceful cad?

"Ah, I see my reputation precedes me, based on the delightful expressions of shock and horror on your faces." Our host smiled devilishly. I did my best to suppress the shiver that worked down my spine. He met the gazes of each of us in the room—at least, those still looking at him. Rose Algernon had her eyes affixed to the floor, and Percy swallowed hard. Lord Asquith tugged at the collar of his starched white shirt. I stepped minutely closer to

Percy, wary of being caught in Horace Barclay's sights. Mr. Harrigan stared at the disgraceful man unflinchingly. I begrudgingly admired his resolve.

"Come now, the mysterious unknown of the games at Mistlethwaite Manor are part of their charm. Did you presume you were invited for a rousing hand of Whist?" He snorted. "Now that one piece of the puzzle—your host—has been made known, I shall acquaint you with the rules of the house." Lord Barclay strutted around the room, the tails of his dinner jacket flapping against the back of his thighs. The man himself was handsome if one could discount his ugly personality and disdainful actions. Approaching his forties, he still retained the vigor of a man in his prime. Though the glint in his dark eyes said he was a man much acquainted with devious intent.

I bit my lip.

"The house rules are fairly simple. Momentarily, I shall read you a little ditty, and the first one of you to solve it shall be the winner of the promised ten thousand pounds." His smile was frigid, showing his slightly crooked front teeth.

Solving a riddle? That didn't sound so horrific. Maybe the feeling of impending dread swirling in my middle was all for naught. Perhaps this weekend wouldn't be an utter disaster after all. Not if I could keep away from Horace Barclay and from Andr—Mr. Harrigan. I swore to distance myself from Mr. Harrigan. There was nothing I could hope to accomplish by remaining in his presence. Indeed, anger and betrayal lingered while my heart still felt bruised. Would that I could shut off my feelings for the man. My fingers curled tighter over Percy's forearm.

Lord Barclay reached inside his dress coat, pulling out a folded piece of heavy paper edged in gilt. He cleared his throat. "Ready for this? The poem is the key.

Two are staff, here to serve,
Our merriment to preserve.

One of you has been bamboozled
One of you is worthless, utterly foozled

One born on the wrong side of the sheets
Two of you, your spouses properly fleeced

For one of you, business has been bad
One of you, your innocence's been had

One of you is a commoner—just polite
One of you a child, innocent not quite

One has been wronged, taken a long fall
Only one is the Master of it all."

He smiled at our shocked faces. Blood drained from my cheeks as the hateful words he spoke registered in my brain.

Who dared to make a mockery of a person's most private moments—of their deepest personal shame? How did he know these things? And which one described *me*?

Percy's arm was so taut, I feared it might snap in half. My heart drummed in my throat, and I felt faint.

"Have you any guesses?" Firelight glinted off his teeth as he smiled wickedly. "Who shall solve my puzzle? The prize money is all yours if you do. Indeed, I have it here in the manor with me. Who will claim it?" He waggled his eyebrows at the silent room, the lot of us apparently still too appalled to respond. "Well, well, this shall be a most entertaining game for me. I trust you all will be turning over in your minds which of your house mates has sins as vile as your own. With that, I leave you all to dinner. I won't join you this time. I grant you one meal to disavow the allegations drawn upon you, but fear not, I shall be most entertained to observe the rest. Perhaps even drop a clue or two to spur someone on to finishing the puzzle.

"However, one last thing to let you have a moment of self-reflection, each of you will draw a piece of paper from this jar, and each of you will take a different route to the dining room where the Leonards will serve you. We have no other staff for the weekend. Just us and them. You are to take this time before dinner in solitary silence to come to terms with yourself and your own errors."

"I will not," Lord Villiers huffed indignantly, though trepidation glimmered in his eyes.

Lord Barclay laughed nonchalantly. "Oh, I think you will, Raymond, my old chap." Lord Villiers bristled at the familiar use of his

Christian name. "If you do not play my game, I shall make
public that which is currently private knowledge. And it won't
be just the guests this weekend. As things stand right now, only
the ten of you here, and my staff and myself of course, know
of this party's collective transgressions, though you are not yet
aware of who has transgressed what. I trust none of you would
like the world at large to know your secret affairs. If you do not
comply, I shall make it my business to inform everyone in all
circles of society of your actions. The papers do so love a juicy
piece of blather. And just think. If I have the power to unearth
such secrets, think how far my reach extends should I desire to
make certain information public." Lord Barclay smiled, slick as
oil.

My stomach turned.

"Now, if you will, please." Lord Barclay held up a glass jar
full of folded papers.

To my surprise, it was Mr. Harrigan who stepped up first,
never once breaking eye contact with Horace The Horrible
Barclay. Mr. Harrigan reached into the jar and withdrew a
folded piece of paper.

Lord Barclay smirked. "Well done, Andrew. You have set a
fine example for the rest."

Mr. Harrigan's knuckles turned white once more as he
gripped his paper and stepped back.

"Don't leave the rest of us in suspense. Tell us where your
starting point is," Lord Barclay insisted.

Andrew's jaw flexed. "The ballroom."

"Excellent choice. And you've already just come through there, so I needn't give you further instruction. If you would wait until all have their papers."

"Lady Hastings, I believe you'll go next." Lord Barclay smiled at me, one eyebrow raised in challenge. I had never felt more like prey than I did in that moment with Horace Barclay's eyes all but undressing me in front of everyone else in the room. Percy stiffened. As I stepped forward Percy gallantly moved with me, refusing to leave my side, for which I was eternally grateful.

Until Lord Barclay put an end to that. "No, no, not you, Percival Crofton. It's not your turn."

I glanced up at Percy, his eyes shadowed with anger, but he stopped, and his arm fell away from beneath my fingers. Swallowing hard, I raised my chin and walked the four paces more to take my turn and pluck out a folded piece of paper.

"The upper art gallery." I read the scripted words aloud.

"An excellent vantage point for spying on the happenings of the ballroom." The lascivious man had the audacity to wink at me. "You'll take the stairs right here at the end of the corridor. Go up, and you'll be in the upper gallery. Now, do note that you may not simply turn and come back down the stairs. You must find the other exit into the dining room. I'll know if you don't. I have eyes all over this house, mind."

The hair on the back of my neck stood on end. But two could play this game. My reputation might depend on it.

"I wouldn't dream of it," I said instead of insulting him with words my mother would faint at hearing. Those I swallowed like bitter lemon, for now.

"Now you, Margaret."

"*Mrs. Wentworth*," she snapped.

"Oh, come, Margaret. We shan't have any hysterics over the weekend. You'll spoil our fun."

Rage boiling over her face, she grabbed a folded paper. "The east salon."

"A glorious room, if ever there was one. It will be cold since the fires aren't lit in that wing of the house. Do be sure to admire the view of the hills if you can see anything beyond this blizzard." Lord Barclay jostled the papers around in his jar then extended the container toward Lord Villiers. "Do have a go, won't you, old chap?"

Lord Villiers seemed to bite back a snarl and dug his hand into the container. "The conservatory."

"A room I should think you'd be most interested in."

Red suffused Lord Villiers's neck.

"Bert, Bert, Bert. Why don't you take a turn?"

The young Lord Asquith was white as a sheet. Indeed, his hand trembled as he tore open his paper. "The b, billiards r, room," he stuttered.

Lord Barclay cawed a harsh laugh. "Oh, I love it. You must enjoy the billiards room while you're there. I'm certain you'll wish to know all its particulars." He turned to the remaining guests. "Lady Algernon. The turn is yours."

The woman's pink gown rustled lightly with the shaking of her arm. Truly, what heinous secrets must Lord Barclay have uncovered? It made me fear for my own secrets—did I have any worth all this? Another thought chilled me to the bone. What if it wasn't a secret directly about me...but something about my family or something that might indirectly affect the course of my life? I could think of one thing in particular that wouldn't be my preference were it exposed...but what if there was something even worse? Lady Algernon still would not meet Lord Barclay's gaze as she drew back her hand.

"The kitchens," she whispered, paper trembling between her fingers.

Lord Barclay clicked his tongue. "I was so hoping you'd draw the guest room."

Her already-wan features paled further. She kept her gaze rooted to the imported rug.

In the end, it was Mr. Angus that drew the guest room. Clarence Campbell drew the armory, and Lady Fulbright drew the library. Lastly, Percy was assigned to the men's smoking lounge.

"You are to remain here until you hear the gong. At the sounding of it, you are to go to your designated areas. Remember the instructions I've given you as how to get there. If you'll draw your attention here by the door, you'll see a blueprint of the manor. You may study it before you go if you feel you must. Also remember that I have eyes and spies all over Mistlethwaite Manor, so do your best not to stray from your place. If you've not appeared after fifteen minutes, Leonard will sound the gong one last time to help you find your way. Follow the clanging. If you still can't find the dining room with that, then you don't deserve to eat. I shall meet you here after dinner, promptly at nine o'clock, for our first round of guesses as to what grievous sins belong to which esteemed guest. Enjoy your meal. It might be the last you ever eat in anonymity."

With a predatory smile, Lord Barclay seated himself in the red velvet chair that matched the draperies, crossed his legs, and steepled his fingers.

CHAPTER FIVE

The clock chimed, and my pulse hammered along my veins. Black dots danced at the edges of my vision for a moment, and I blinked to clear them. The gong sounded, not ten seconds after the clock chimed. They were nothing in this house if not punctual.

"Let the games begin! I'll be waiting." Lord Barclay's lips twitched in private amusement.

Lying in wait more like.

Wretched Cretin.

I glanced at Percy. He swallowed and gave me a strained smile. As I was turning toward the door, I caught Mr. Harrigan's gaze. He held it a moment, nodded briefly then ducked into the hallway.

"I'll see you in a few moments," Percy whispered as he passed me and made his exit. I nodded, mustered my courage, then stepped into the chilly hallway to face my fate.

The corridor to the ballroom was short. The steps to the upper gallery should be just beyond. I risked a look over my shoulder, wondering if Andr—Mr. Harrigan—had quit the room yet and headed to the ballroom. I didn't see him. It didn't matter anyway. I gripped my skirt in both my hands and made my way to the steep, winding steps that would lead me to my assigned destination.

My lace flounce rustled against the marble steps, the black veining in the white stone reminding me of poison spreading through something pure. Much like the situation in which I currently found myself. Something that had been such an untainted occasion—a propitious occasion that might've raised my status yet now licked at me like the flaming tongues of the underworld.

I shuddered and gripped the green silk of my skirts tighter as the words of Lord Barclay's poem bounced around inside my skull.

Every word of the hateful poem was burned with intensity into my brain. Possessing a vivid memory was both blessing and curse. I could call to mind nearly every word spoken if I paid attention, but it also meant every word Andrew Harrigan had ever whispered to me was etched in my mind. Percy's words were there, too, but he was partial more to smiles and flirtatious looks and given less to words themselves.

Words, it seemed, were destined to stick with me.

Thinking of both men as I reached the top of the stairway, I came to the first of a series of arched openings that looked down upon the ballroom. It would have been a glorious vantage from which to watch ladies in their swirling silks and men in their tails, twirling in time to live musicians hidden artfully in the gallery. I could just make it out on the opposite side from where I now stood.

I surveyed the darkened great hall that doubled as the ballroom. Enough light from the low-turned gas lights illuminated the black and white tiled floor, shined onto the gilt statuary built into the walls, and gave me enough visibility between the heavy shadows of the arches to see to the end of the hallway. But the light did not reveal Andrew Harrigan. I fully expected to see him crossing the floor at the same time I walked across the upper gallery. Glancing down the extensive gallery, the long-dead eyes of past Mistlethwaite masters stared down at me. Their painted eyes were far too life-like for my liking, and I was again reminded of Lord Barclay's words. Eyes all over Mistlethwaite indeed.

Suppressing a shiver, I confessed to myself it would have been comforting had I heard Mr. Harrigan's footsteps echoing my own. I would have felt no less cross with him but would have felt less alone. But as something must have kept him, I quickened my pace to a fast clip down the gallery. I was done having dead men stare at me.

Two wrong turns later and no closer to discerning my line in the horrid riddle, I found my way into the dining room, thanks to the savory scents of roasted meat and Christmas spices.

An enormous stuffed turkey dominated the grand table, its golden skin crisp and glistening. Deep gravy boats full of tempting giblet sauce orbited the silver dish heaped high with roasted root vegetables. Small plates of pickles, olives, celery, and corn dotted the table, flanked by two towering platters of tiny mince pies. Miniature animals made of marzipan hunched over candied nuts.

The room was well lit but only one other guest had beat me to the space. William Angus stood, hands clasped behind his back, as he stared at the enormous painting of Horace The Horrible Barclay that graced the space above the impressive mantle. The painter had been most gracious; it was a good likeness and held none of the man's malice.

"Ah, Lady Hastings." The man's subtle brogue was a pleasant undercurrent to his voice. "I see you've made it to the dining room. Any troubles?" His dark eyes reflected the fire, and I was reminded of those flames of the underworld.

I cleared my throat, attempting to project a serene mask to cover my wildly churning emotions. "None at all. Yourself, sir?" I asked politely.

He shook his head. "Had you any inkling this was to be the turn of events?"

"Not in the slightest. Did you?"

He shook his head once more and turned back to the fire.

Just then, Clarence Campbell sauntered in. I was beginning to think the man didn't walk so much as he slunk. There was something about him that set my teeth on edge—beyond whatever heinous things he might have done, according to Lord Barclay. I clasped my hands in front of me, nervously twisting the opal ring on my right hand. I hoped I'd soon have a diamond on my left.

Where was Percy? Had he somehow managed to get lost on his way here? I expected him to be one of the first ones here since he hadn't terribly far to go. A shriek howled down the hallway, followed by a gust of wind through the dining room doors. A flurry of snow pounded against the tall windows on the opposite side of the room.

As if mere thoughts could conjure him, Percy bustled over the threshold, snow clinging to his hair and shoulders.

"Lord Fairfax?" I asked as I quickly crossed to him. Clutching his sleeve, I dragged him closer to the hearth. "What on earth happened?"

"The door flung open, doused me in snow and has quite chilled me to the bone. I had to go out in the blizzard to get the doors shut." His hands were cold and wet.

"Here, man. Come warm yourself," Mr. Angus said, moving aside and motioning to the roaring blaze.

"What was that dreadful noise?" Mrs. Wentworth said as she hurried in, rubbing her hands over her upper arms. Belatedly, I realized my shawl was gone. Perhaps I dropped it in my shock over Lord Barclay's words. I suddenly missed its slight weight against my shoulders.

"Door blew open." Percy's teeth chattered as he extended his hands to warm them.

Lord Asquith strode through the doors, his earlier cheerful demeanor replaced by a false brightness.

"I say down with all the balderdash this fellow is spewing. Let's have drinks and make this a proper holiday party!" Without waiting for anyone else, the young man walked with purpose to the sideboard and poured himself a liberal helping of spirits. My eyes widened as he tossed his head back and swigged deeply.

"Steady on, man. You'll be blootered before dinner is even on the plates," Mr. Campbell said, eyebrow raised in disdain. The young Lord Asquith couldn't be but a year or two older than me at most, but he drank like a fish.

"A real man knows how to hold his liquor," Lord Villiers declared as he came through the door.

Another tense moment was broken as Lady Algernon made her appearance, followed quickly by Lady Fulbright.

Where was Mr. Harrigan?

He had the same amount of distance to come as I did—so where was he? I glanced at the clock. His fifteen minutes were up. The gong sounded from its hidden alcove, and I shuddered. The bellow of the metal reverberated in my bones.

"Where is Mr. Harrigan?" Mrs. Wentworth asked, her perusal harsh and judgmental.

"Clearly, he isn't here," Lady Fulbright said with a roll of her eyes.

The gong sounded again and the hairs on the back of my neck stood on end.

"Do you suppose he got lost?" Percy asked, his face still pale, eyes troubled.

"He shouldn't have—he had only to cross the great hall," I said softly.

Just then, the man's caramel-colored hair flashed in the doorway. Andrew took in the assembled room and dipped his head. "Apologies. Took a wrong turn." He smiled ruefully, though I noticed his eyes did not crinkle. He was as on edge as the rest of us.

A gasp escaped Lady Algernon's lips as the butler Leonard appeared as if out of nowhere, from behind a heavy green damask curtain. The scents of pine and cinnamon wafted with the material.

"If you all will take your seats, Mrs. Leonard and I will serve." He gave a half bow, somehow adding gravity rather than formality to the occasion. "You'll note the place cards."

I hadn't studied the table too closely beyond the decadent feast until now, too anxious over everyone's arrival. I gave the settings themselves my attention. Little gilt place cards sat at the head of each plate, next to the wine and water glasses.

I had to admire the skill with which the table had been laid. Though incorrectly labeled as to the societal positions of the guests, the place settings were affixed to perfection by the miniature cake stands behind them—each little stand holding a miniature three-tiered cake decorated with sugar paste pinecones, greenery, and studded with little red currants. Pity I had no appetite.

"This is utterly incorrect," Lady Fulbright said. She stood at the end of the table. "I cannot be placed here. I outrank at least eight of you present." She sniffed airily.

"Oh, do give it up," Mrs. Wentworth said coyly.

"You would say that, as you are seated at the head of the table opposite Lord Villiers," Lady Fulbright snapped.

William Angus in his cheap black suit sat himself without fanfare next to where Mrs. Wentworth stood. She froze, her mouth agape at the sight of the man so far below her stature seated so nonchalantly.

He glanced up at her. "It would seem, Madame, that we are all equal in the eyes of our host."

I bit the inside of my cheek. He was right. I found my assigned place—midway down the table and seated between Lord Asquith and Mr. Campbell. Directly across from Andrew Harrigan, so that I could not help but gaze into his brown eyes every time I lifted my head. Percy sat one seat down from him, Rose Algernon between them, where Percy would be forced to see me repeatedly look at my former fiancé.

My guts twisted. This was yet another ploy of our host to make us on edge and uncomfortable. If he knew our collective dark secrets, he surely knew about my past with Andr—Mr. Harrigan and was clearly trying to use it to his advantage. It was certain to sow jealousy and discord between Percy and me if I let it. Refusing to rise to the horrible man's bait, I rested my eyes on the table, only to find a card sticking out from beneath my plate. Tugging it out, I nearly dropped it.

It was the hateful poem.

Two are staff, here to serve,
Our merriment to preserve.

One of you has been bamboozled
One of you is worthless, utterly foozled

One born on the wrong side of the sheets
Two of you, your spouses properly fleeced

For one of you, business has been bad
One of you, your innocence's been had

One of you is a commoner—just polite
One of you a child, innocent not quite

One has been wronged, taken a long fall
Only one is the Master of it all.

I wanted to crush it between my fingers.

Christmas Games 1895

Two are staff, here to serve,
Our merriment to preserve.

One of you has been bamboozled
One of you is worthless, utterly foozled

One born on the wrong side of the sheets
Two of you, your spouses properly fleeced

For one of you, business has been bad
One of you, your innocence's been had

One of you is a commoner—just polite
One of you a child, innocent not quite

One has been wronged, taken a long fall
Only one is the Master of it all.

"I will not stand for this." Lord Villiers had found his card as well. He charged to his feet and thrust his poem into the crackling hearth. "There is no merit to these words."

"Or too much, as it certainly seems to have struck a chord," Mr. Campbell chimed beside me.

"If we do not play his game, there is nothing he can do about it," Mrs. Wentworth said primly.

"Unless he makes good on his threat to make hidden things public," Mr. Harrigan said quietly as his eyes wandered over the assembled guests. His words struck true as silence fell over the table. He met my eyes unflinchingly. I swallowed and looked away.

"First course. Please enjoy." Leonard opened another hidden door from the paneling and Mrs. Leonard wheeled a cart in. On beautiful white china plates sat an array of raw oysters in their native casings. Leonard efficiently placed a plate of them in front of each of us, the smaller china plates making soft clinks against the larger charger plates beneath them.

The gelatinous meat stared balefully up at me from its half shell. My stomach turned and I took a quick swallow of water. I wouldn't go near the wine, not even to calm my racing nerves. I had a premonition that I would need all my wits about me to survive this weekend unscathed.

But truly, which of the lines of the poem was about me? I had secrets—of course I had secrets. Everyone had things private they did not want shared with the rest of the world. My gaze flitted over the card once more. Blood rushed to my face as I thought over the implications of each line. And which ones might apply to me...one in particular I feared.

It was the longest dinner of my life.

CHAPTER SIX

The meal had been stilted at best. Small talk, biting remarks, shifting eyes, and the scrape of cutlery against bone china had been the course of the evening. I'd said little, eaten even less, and was ready to go home.

Part of me was terrified that Lord Barclay knew something about my past that I did not...and that I did not want brought to light. Father was much older than Mother...but surely, I was the product of both my parents? I cast the awful thought aside. Another part of me feared he knew exactly what secret I wanted kept hidden. Shame curdled the little bit of dinner I'd managed to consume.

We walked as one group, our party hushed, trepidation's foot-falls sounding heavy beside our own as we made our way back toward the great hall. Heaven forbid we miss coffee with our odious host. Whereupon reaching our destination, I was certain he'd make us go around the circle, guessing each other's secret sins.

My hand was tucked in the crook of Percy's elbow. It could have been merely the vibrations of our steps, but I thought his arm trembled slightly. Perhaps he was as nervous as I was. But surely, Percival Crofton could have nothing so horrible that he'd be ashamed for me to know, could he? Though I had one thing in particular I wished him not to know...

The words of the poem drummed against my skull.

I felt Mr. Harrigan's presence behind me. It both comforted me and unsettled me to have him so near, and I cursed my fickle emotions. Why could I not leave Andrew Harrigan in my past?

Mrs. Wentworth had insisted on going first. She was certainly uppity enough for her lower social position—which, if rumor were to be trusted, even that was serving her little in her current circumstances. Beside her was the young Lord Asquith, his halting steps showing his agitation and his earlier consumption of more alcohol than was advisable.

The two of them disappeared through the threshold into the beckoning light of the room where we'd first met with Lord Barclay. Suddenly, there was a loud crash and a scream that cut straight to my marrow.

I yanked my arm from Percy's grasp and darted ahead. Arriving at the doorway, several things registered at once.

The first was Mrs. Wentworth's shrieking blaring in my ears like the wailing of a banshee. The second was Lord Asquith retching up the contents of his stomach into an antique Grecian urn. The third made my blood freeze.

There, face down and unmoving against the patterned carpet, was Horace Barclay. With a knife sticking out of his back.

"Come away." The voice was low, and the hand on my arm was gentle. So distraught at what my brain tried to comprehend, my vision grew fuzzy until I blinked and found myself several paces away, near the alcove where I'd first grabbed Andrew's sleeve. Turning my head, brown eyes met mine, not blue ones.

"Andrew?" Why was my head so foggy?

"Don't look, Emma Grace. Turn to me." His face was pale. Things clicked into place in a great rush. I did look back then, despite the warning against it. Looked at the gore of what was left of our host, then let my gaze encompass each one of the Mistlethwaite visitants.

The poem.

The accusations.

The guests.

The dead body.

If what Lord Barclay had implied in his hateful little ditty was true, then every single guest here had a motive to kill the man.

Solving the Mistlethwaite holiday puzzle took on new meaning as I realized I could be looking at Lord Barclay's killer. I gripped my skirt as black dots spangled the edges of my vision, took a deep breath through my nose, and blew it out slowly through my lips.

"Emma Grace, are you well?" Percy's voice broke into my shattered thoughts. He glared heatedly at Andrew until he stepped back, relinquishing his place beside me so that Percy might take over my comfort.

My fists left my skirt and gripped Percy's forearms instead. "Percy, tell me this is a horrible dream."

"I—I wish I could." Glancing up, I saw that Percy's face was pale and sweating. I feared he may soon be as sick as Lord Asquith.

"Great Scot!" William Angus blurted as we all stood around the body.

I fought around a surge of nausea to maintain my equilibrium then forced my emotions down, determined to think through things logically and rationally...and not give in to the hysteria clawing at my corset to get out.

"Who has done this?" Lady Algernon cried. I was unsure if the sparkle in her eyes was distress or hidden glee. Maybe both?

"Saints preserve us," Mrs. Wentworth mumbled, staring distastefully at the body.

Mr. Campbell whistled through his teeth.

Lord Asquith, pale and ashen, wiped the back of his hand across his mouth. "That certainly puts a damper on the party."

"A permanent one for Lord Barclay, it would seem," Percy rasped, eyes riveted on the knife protruding from the lower right region of Lord Barclay's back.

"I agree with Lady Algernon. Speak. Who has done this?" Lord Villiers said, crossing his arms and standing like a giant sentinel in the middle of the room.

"For all we know, it was *you*," William Angus said, a defiant tilt to his left eyebrow.

Lord Villiers stuttered. "Why, you impudent little—"

"Peace, gentlemen, please. There are ladies present," Percy intoned, his voice still strained.

"Not to mention the dead man," Mr. Harrigan quipped.

Percy shot him a withering glare.

"Where are Mr. and Mrs. Leonard?" Lady Fulbright asked. Her head whipped around as if searching for hidden intruders.

"Quite right. We should send for them at once. We must ascertain if there are more staff present—despite Lord Barclay's earlier insinuations. There could be a hidden killer amongst us. We must alert the authorities at once," Percy said with great adamance. He left my side and rang the bell on the wall to call for the staff.

"How do you suggest we reach the authorities?" Mr. Harrigan asked. He was turned toward the long window. Outside was a mass of blackest night and white fury as snow pounded against the windows, howling to gain entrance and snuff out the warmth of the room. Though the fire was hot enough, a dead chill wrapped tentacles around my heart.

"Maybe they have a telephone nearby?" Lady Fulbright offered.

"And a fine time we'd have getting to it tonight," Mr. Angus said. "Regardless of what we find tonight, we must all remain here, indoors." *With each other* was implied at the end of his sentence.

Lady Fulbright gulped as she took in the snow pounding against the windows. "You don't think we—we could go for help?"

"Don't be foolish," Lord Villiers said gruffly. "You'd be lost within one foot of the door and freeze to death not long after."

We were trapped until the storm let up.

"You. You were the last to the table," Mrs. Wentworth pointed an accusing finger at Andrew. My heart lurched; I'd had the same thoughts.

Andrew crossed his arms over his chest. "We all of us started from various places in the manor. Any one of us had time to double back, kill Lord Barclay, then make it to the dining room."

"But you were gone the longest and had the shortest starting point," Mrs. Wentworth insisted.

"Indeed, what's he got on you?" Lord Villiers turned angry eyes to Andrew.

My throat constricted. This was getting out of hand. We'd have a proper witch hunt soon at the rate we were going.

"Do you know which line of the poem pertains to you? Perhaps your motivation is stronger than mine," Andrew said evenly.

Lord Villiers swallowed, faltering slightly.

Andrew lifted an eyebrow—a silent challenge.

"Gentlemen, please. This will solve nothing," Percy intoned, mopping his brow.

"Or discovering the poem's secrets will solve *everything*," Andrew said softly.

Someone swore.

"I suppose you'd like to go first?" Lady Fulbright said, lips pinched tight.

"It's hardly a secret that my family has fallen from grace." Andrew smiled ruefully. "Would you care to spill your secrets, Lady Fulbright?" Andrew glanced from her to Lord Villiers and red suffused her cheeks.

Oh, heavens. Could they be the ones fleecing their spouses? Were they having an affair *together*? Was that why they'd both been invited to Mistlethwaite Manor?

"Why you, you only think your family is ruined now! I'll make you rue the day you inherited your empty title! How dare you besmirch my good name in such a fashion," spluttered Lord Villiers.

"It's not as if it's any great offense when those among the nobility have affairs," Mr. Campbell threw in, almost bored.

"I—I am not having an affair with this woman!" Lord Villiers practically roared.

Lady Fulbright seemed to shrink into herself, tears fringing her lower lids.

"Lady Hastings then?" Mr. Campbell tossed out, looking pointedly at me.

I gasped in horror. "I most certainly am not!"

"Pray then, you've been awfully quiet. What grievous sin have you committed on Lord Barclay's list?" Lord Asquith said, taking a sudden interest in the conversation.

Anxiety churned in my gut as bile rose in the back of my throat. I swallowed hard, shame, confusion, and anger sinking claws into my midsection. Straightening, Andrew uncrossed his arms, glaring at Lord Asquith. Percy crossed the room to stand near me, wrapping my hand into the crook of his elbow.

"What a pack of wolves you are!" Percy snapped.

"I don't know which line pertains to me," I confessed in a strangled whisper.

"Committed a multitude of sins, then, have we?" Mr. Angus said.

I glowered at him.

A shocked curse dropped from the doorway.

Mr. and Mrs. Leonard stood at the threshold, staring in horror at the body on the floor.

"Where were you right before dinner?" Lady Algernon wasted no time interrogating the staff.

"Readying to serve the meal, of course," Mr. Leonard retorted. Mrs. Leonard crossed herself as if to ward off evil.

"Are there any other staff members here for the weekend? Who else is in the manor?" Percy asked, taking charge once more.

Leonard shook his head. "N-no one. The only ones present for the entire weekend are here in this room. And judging by the storm, even if someone else had wanted to enter, they could not have. I personally answered the door to gain each of you your admittance, and the door has been locked in between and double checked once the final guest arrived."

"Didn't you say the door blew open?" Mr. Angus asked Percy.

"I did. You must not have locked it well." Percy's lips thinned as he looked condescendingly at Leonard.

Leonard's mouth opened and shut with no sound issuing forth. "I, I did. I locked it tight; I swear. It bolts from the inside."

"How did you come to work for Lord Barclay?" Mr. Campbell asked.

The two servants glanced at each other.

"Well, out with it!" thundered Lord Villiers, his gray-streaked hair shining in the gas light.

"Are you here under your own compulsion, or were you coerced?" Mr. Harrigan asked.

Mr. Leonard took a stuttering breath. "We..."

"We once tried to steal from an employer," Mrs. Leonard blurted.

Leonard glared at his wife as the room descended once more into a suffocating hush.

"What do we do now?" Lady Algernon whispered into the thick tension. Her pink skirt had wrinkles set into it where she'd clutched at it.

"We cannot leave the man lying on the floor with a knife sticking out of him." Mr. Angus said.

"Where do you propose we take him?" This from Lord Villiers, sarcasm heavy in his voice.

"Where's the nearest bedchamber?" Andrew inquired of Leonard.

"There is a study with a couch at the end of this hallway, otherwise, the closest bedroom is on the guest level up three flights of stairs."

"I have no wish to sleep in a room near the dead." Mrs. Wentworth shuddered.

"You plan to sleep?" Lady Fulbright asked.

"Perhaps she is the murderer and has no need to fear the villain will come for her," Mr. Campbell said.

"You will not speak thusly to me!" Mrs. Wentworth screeched.

"And who's going to stop me? I'll say what I please, and to whomever I please," Mr. Campbell shot back. Red crept up his neck.

Lord Asquith tossed back another shot of strong drink from the sideboard in the far corner of the room.

Percy pinched the bridge of his nose. "Right. Stop bickering. Let's move Mr., er, the body to the study and then go to bed. Perhaps things will have cleared in the morning, and we can leave this hellish nightmare."

He spoke sense, and the accusations stopped flying, though there were plenty of heated glares circling the room.

"Well, move him then," Lord Villiers demanded.

"Go right ahead, old man," Lord Asquith said, his eyes still glassy.

"Shut up, both of you," Andrew said. "Leonard, grab his feet."

"I..." Leonard started. "My dear, run ahead and turn up the lights so we might see," he said to his wife.

"Wait. Someone go with her. No one should go anywhere alone," Mr. Angus said, moving to block the door.

"Go on then, go with her," Mrs. Wentworth said, shooing her hand toward them.

"Mrs. Wentworth, you go as well. The three of you go turn up the lights, the rest of us will follow the...body." Percy stumbled over the word.

Truly, the whole thing was such a monstrous disaster.

Mr. Angus frowned and twitched his head to Mrs. Wentworth. With much huffing and grumbling, and possibly a muffled unladylike oath or two, she complied. The three of them—Mrs. Wentworth, Mrs. Leonard, and Mr. Angus all went ahead to light the lamps while the rest of us clumped helplessly around Andrew and Leonard as they hoisted the dead Lord Barclay to take him from the room.

I was too distracted to look for my shawl.

CHAPTER SEVEN

T he collective rooms were silent as the grave. I shuddered, forcing images of Lord Barclay's body from my mind. When they picked him up, the knife had shifted, and fresh blood had welled around the weapon. Blood had dripped down the hallway as he was moved.

After that, there was nothing more to do than to trudge to the third level and to our rooms. We all walked up as one mass, everyone on edge, trusting no one.

"I'll escort you to your door," Percy said, his voice strained. My footfalls were muffled against the carpet runner that graced the hardwood floors.

We reached the darkened doorway and it creaked open with a gentle push. My stomach flipped. I hadn't felt the need to secure it earlier, but I'd most assuredly be locking it from here on out.

"I'll bid you good night then. I'll see you in the morning." He smiled—or at least attempted a smile. His eyes were troubled, lines appearing at their corners and creases across his forehead even as his lips curved upward.

He leaned over, clasping my hand and drawing it to his lips. My insides squirmed as I realized we had an audience. About half of the guests still stood in the hallway, observing our display of affection. Blood rushed to my cheeks.

"If either of you were married, I'd say for certain you were the ones fleecing your spouses," Mr. Campbell said dryly.

I cringed, tearing my hand from Percy's grasp.

"Hold your tongue." Percy growled the words. He stalked down the hallway to his room and all but slammed his door shut.

I wasted no time and slipped inside my own, turning the knob on the gas light as high as I dared, throwing illumination into all corners of the ornate room. Even so, there were too many shadows for my comfort.

A soft knock sounded at the door at my back, and I jumped, a tiny squeal escaping my lips.

"Emma Grace, it's Andrew," came a whisper.

Feeling equal parts trepidation and excitement at hearing Andrew's voice, I cracked the door, not daring to open it wider. I was, after all, still an unmarried young woman, and circumstances notwithstanding, I did still have my reputation to consider.

"Emma Grace," he repeated, his voice low and rough. "Wedge a chair under your doorknob tonight."

"What?" That wasn't what I expected him to say, and my brain was having trouble keeping up. I cracked the door wider. "Of course, I'll lock my door."

He shook his head. "No. Wedge a chair as well. There could be a master key. Locking your door might not be enough."

I blinked slowly and took a shaky breath. I nodded, the full import of his words sinking in. "I will."

"Do you need anything? You are well enough given the circumstances?"

"I am. Thank you for your concern."

"Emma—" He didn't finish, just drifted off, searching my face. I felt exposed. Exposed in a way I didn't like. Like Andrew Harrigan could see all my secrets—both those I kept only to myself...and the one he shared with me.

Wind howled outside, the chill air blowing in through the cracks around the stained-glass windows and sending a shiver over my shoulders.

"You took the longest to get to the dining room." The words dropped into the heavy silence between us.

He frowned. "Yes." He drew the word out, suspicion lacing his words.

I bit the inside of my cheek, screwing up my courage. I didn't make a habit of accusing men of murder, but some baser part of my nature *needed* to know if Andrew had done the deed. "You had motive. Horace Barclay ruined your life. Ruined your family."

He reeled back like I'd slapped him.

There was a moment of tense silence that permeated the darkness.

Andrew's brown eyes bored into mine. "Emma Grace, I did not kill anyone. Do you truly think me capable of murder?"

I shivered again—from an entirely different cause. "Mr. Harrigan, I think *everyone* is capable of murder, given the right circumstances. And you had motive. Motive of which I'm certain." Pain echoed in my chest as the words left my mouth.

Andrew dragged a hand through his hair and blew a sigh out. "As far as we know, if Barclay's words are to be trusted, every person here has motive—right down to the staff—if he held sway over them the way he has secrets on the rest of us. But let us note the difference between murder and killing. Murder implies forethought and intent, does it not? I don't disagree with you, Lady Hastings." The use of my formal name on his lips sent another chill skipping down my spine. "I don't disagree that *everyone* is capable of *killing*—I'd kill in an instant if it meant keeping you safe. But I tell you the truth"—he looked me in the eye— "when I say I did not murder Horace Barclay. I cannot pretend that his death has saddened me because it certainly has not. I *am*, however, yet concerned for your safety."

"Did you *kill* him, then?" The words were a hush of terrified whisper, even as warmth coiled in my belly.

A bitter half smile twitched the corner of his lips. "No, Emma Grace. I did not kill, nor did I murder, Horace Barclay."

I searched his face. His eyes remained locked on mine, one eyebrow raised.

"Do you believe me?" His words were a low rumble of thunder across my skin.

"I'm not sure," I answered honestly.

He blew a hot breath out and stepped back from my doorway.

"Brace your door, Lady Hastings. I bid you good night."

"Good night." I closed the door, heart pounding. Glancing to my left, I saw a delicate, satin seated chair. I grabbed it without further thought, jammed it beneath the handle of the doorknob, and flipped the deadbolt.

CHAPTER EIGHT

I stared into my shadow-shrouded room and swallowed hard. Andrew's words had shaken me. Did I truly think he murdered—killed—Lord Barclay? He had motive. *Strong* motive. Horace Barclay had thrown the entire Harrigan family into the dirt. They had no hope of recovering their family's wealth. Coming here, to Mistlethwaite Manor, seeing all the trappings of opulence, of what his family must once have enjoyed without thought, only to realize that the Harrigan fortune had likely supplied the funds for this weekend's festivities and purchased who knows what other frivolities? It must have shaken Andre—Mr. Harrigan.

Hang it all.

It must have shaken *Andrew*.

The indignity of it boiled my own blood.

I thought of old Lady Harrigan. Sitting alone, clothed in black, huddled on her favorite divan in front of a fire, mourning the loss of her family's fortune, her family's stature, and more so, mourning the loss of her devoted husband.

I screwed my eyes shut as regret bloomed in my chest. Andrew's father had taken the shock of their loss badly. So badly that he'd suffered a heart seizure and had passed away within a fortnight of their fortune crumbling. I had attended the wake, tried to comfort Andrew, but he'd pushed me away. Three days after the funeral, he'd cut all ties with me, breaking our engagement, and shattering my heart along with it.

A sob somersaulted up my throat and I viciously held it back behind my teeth. It had been over a year since Lord Hastings had gone to glory, and over a year since I'd seen Andrew Harrigan. I should have asked after his family—his mother and his younger sisters. With his father's passing, the mantle of responsibility had fallen solely to Andrew. It would have at least been polite of me to inquire after them. I missed them. His sister Agnes had been a close friend of mine. When our engagement was called off, it wasn't just a fiancé that I lost. I lost friends. I lost the man I'd loved. I lost the future I'd desperately wanted.

I swiped beneath my eyes, refusing to submit to the indignity of tears. Surely it was this wretched situation playing havoc with my emotions. Anyone would be notably upset and unsettled having witnessed what I had this evening.

Leaving my place against the door, I assured myself the chair was wedged securely beneath the knob, then walked to my trunk.

Should I change into my sleeping gown and attempt to rest? I glanced around the room again. Might as well. Even though prickles of apprehension danced along my scalp, there was no way anyone could enter my bed chambers with the door so securely locked and barred. Snow and ice pounded against the glass of the window, some stories above the ground, and a warm fire was still alight in the hearth.

I took off my fine green dress, draping it gently over the back of the chair stationed at the small writing desk. Wind howled outside, the shriek of it raking down my spine and breaking goose flesh out all over my arms. I turned to unlace my corset nearer the warm fire, but a square of paper caught my attention, positioned at the edge of the desk.

Leaning over, I tugged the paper from beneath the glass orb weight.

"Detestable verse," I muttered, face drawing into a scowl as I realized I held a printed version of Lord Barclay's poem. I thought to toss it into the flames as Lord Villiers had his at the dinner table, but a thought struck.

It was Andrew that had said solving the poem might solve everything—meaning the murder. If we discovered who had the strongest motivations for silencing our host, would that provide us with the culprit?

I shivered again in the chilliness of the room and put the card back down on the desk. After shimmying out of my corset and into my lacy night dress and warm, velvet dressing gown, I grabbed a quill and ink bottle, the poem, and a few sheets of paper. Nudg-

ing the wingback chair closer to the fire and moving the little
end table closer as well, I stared at the poem, turning over all the
exchanged words of the evening in relation to who each line of
the poem might refer.

Two are staff, here to serve,
Our merriment to preserve.

One of you has been bamboozled
One of you is worthless, utterly foozled

One born on the wrong side of the sheets
Two of you, your spouses properly fleeced

For one of you, business has been bad
One of you, your innocence's been had

One of you is a commoner—just polite
One of you a child, innocent not quite

One has been wronged, taken a long fall
Only one is the Master of it all.

Clearly the two staff were Mr. and Mrs. Leonard. I scratched
their names beside the top two lines. I thought there was a good
chance Lord Villiers was having an affair. Likely with Lady Ful-

bright, given their reactions. I penned their names in next to the line about fleeced spouses.

My heart pinched as I glanced over the other stanzas. Was it Andrew that had been bamboozled? From what I'd heard, the deal that had been struck in good faith was clearly underhanded, meant to steal the Harrigan's fortune and benefit only Lord Barclay. But why would Lord Barclay do such a thing? Was the old Lord Stanford—Andrew's father—simply an easy mark? Was there something else behind it? Was Andrew associated with his father's error in judgment in the poem? Andrew was far from worthless, but could the actions of their shoddy deal make him foozled?

Heat flooded my cheeks as my eyes skimmed the rest of the poem. I gripped the pen hard enough my fingers shook, dripping a splotch next to the line about innocence lost. An English girl of the aristocracy was supposed to reach her wedding day completely pure—no stain upon her. And while I wasn't ashamed of my past actions exactly, I did regret them now that I was set to marry into the Fairfax lineage. Percy kissing my hand in the hallway was tantamount to a marriage proposal—and as I was certain he'd be offering a proper one, it was the only reason I allowed such intimacies. Percy was the sort of man who would expect a stainless bride. One whose lips had been held in reserve.

Christmas Games 1895

Two are staff, here to serve,
Our merriment to preserve. *Mr. and Mrs. Leonard*

One of you has been bamboozled
One of you is worthless, utterly foozled

One born on the wrong side of the sheets
Two of you, your spouses properly fleeced *Lord Villiers and Lady Fulbright*

For one of you, business has been bad
One of you, your innocence's been had

One of you is a commoner—just polite
One of you a child, innocent not quite

One has been wronged, taken a long fall
Only one is the Master of it all.

But Andrew...I'd let Andrew kiss me full on the mouth. Only once. But still. My fingers strayed to my lips, my memory betraying me and playing the moment over and over.

We'd been in the garden at his family's estate, strolling in the pleasant fall sunshine. The leaves were turning, and the air was crisp with promise. Andrew's ring sparkled on my finger. My hand was tucked into the crook of his elbow, our legs brushing together as we walked. Euphoria bubbled in my chest as we rounded the bend into the maze, the boxwood hedges a foot taller than we were, completely obscuring us from his sisters and our mothers as they all chatted happily on the lawn over by a cultivated patch of aster flowers.

We paused as if by some mutual unspoken agreement as a light breeze toyed with the curls around my face. Andrew gently pushed one back behind my ear and my knees felt like festive jelly that bobbled all over.

"Emma Grace," he whispered. His brown eyes crinkled with the width of his smile, his face wreathed in sunshine and hope as he gazed down at me.

"Andrew," I whispered back.

"I'm in love with you," he confessed quietly, his smile falling, replaced with sincerity. Andrew had never said those words to me before.

My knees thoroughly wobbled then.

His hand carefully cupped the curve of my waist with enough pressure to be certain I wasn't tumbling to the earth. Mine landed on his chest. His eyes widened, and mine probably did, too. Such intimate touching was utterly foreign, and it felt like champagne was fizzing inside me. Andrew swallowed, his gaze dipping to my mouth. My breathing all but stopped, air coming into my lungs with quick, tight gasps.

Andrew cleared his throat and made to step back, but my hand fisted into the lapel of his jacket.

"I love you, too."

The sunshine smile spread across his face once more and my world shifted—Andrew became my axis in that moment.

My eyes fixed on his lips, my own parting with the knowledge that all the feelings bottled up inside me were reciprocated—that my soon-to-be-husband wanted me as I wanted him.

His thumb traced the curve of my jaw with a familiarity we had only begun to discover.

My eyelids fluttered shut and I savored the moment. Too soon, his hand fell away.

"I want to kiss you in the worst way," he admitted, a roguish but rueful smile tipping the corner of his mouth.

"Then you should," I whispered as that fizzing champagne exploded inside me.

He blinked, searching my eyes. "Are you certain?"

I smiled. Andrew had never been anything but the perfect gentleman.

"I'm certain."

Needing no second prompting, with great reverence, Andrew's fingers skimmed my jaw again, reaching back to cradle the back of my head. I tipped my face, eager for his kiss.

Light as butterfly wings, Andrew's lips closed over mine. They were soft, warm, and full of promise. Something inside me released with that first kiss—a part of me I willingly gave to Andrew—a part of me that no one else could ever have because I'd given it to him.

He took the gift I offered, treasuring it, and gave me part of himself in return. When we broke apart, my soul felt older, wiser, and cherished. And tethered to the man in front of me.

Three weeks later I was a broken woman with a wrecked engagement, and a part of me was gone that I could never recall.

On top of our shattered engagement, I felt ruined. That first kiss should have gone to the man I married. And instead, it would always belong to Andrew Harrigan.

The fire crackled, breaking me from my reverie. Absently, I noted the tears silently making their way down my cheeks.

Angrily, I scrubbed at them, but they welled afresh as I glanced again at the poem.

Was I the child, innocent not quite?

A single kiss in a garden maze was hardly ammunition enough to warrant the murder of a man, though I highly doubted Percy or his family would be impressed with my actions. It would be humiliating, certainly, if my indiscretion was discovered. Unless Lord Barclay knew something about the Croftons' expectations of their son's bride that I did not.

My tears stopped as ice lodged in my throat.

What if Percy's parents put a stop to our impending engagement because my shared kiss with Andrew made me tainted in their eyes?

That would not be good. Not at all.

I was fast approaching the age where men would pass over me in lieu of younger women, or in favor of an American heiress instead. My dowry was sizeable enough, I was well bred, had a titled father, and all the right societal connections. But the clock was working against me. My engagement with Andrew had been arranged early on—I'd never needed to look at another young man—never wanted to if I was completely honest. But when that arrangement had been ripped from me, it left me aged and dangling over a void. A void I immediately needed to fill with suitors and a proposal, lest advancing age cause me to fall into that abyss without a suitor to catch me.

I scrubbed my hands down my face, shaking such mind-tangling thoughts from my head, and resolved to rest as best I was able. Shrugging out of my robe and shimmying into the bed, I pulled the thick down comforter up to my ears and let myself drift into fitful sleep.

I should have stayed awake.

CHAPTER NINE

I 'd left the gas lamps on low upon going to bed. I couldn't bring myself to extinguish them completely and leave myself alone in the darkness. As such, even though the devastating snowstorm blocked most of the dawn's light, my room was still plenty lit enough that the first thing I saw when I cracked my eyes open was a single red rose in a vase atop the papers I'd left on the table by the wingbacked chair.

A rose and vase that had not been present in my room the night before.

A scream built in my chest and had leaped from my lips before I'd made the conscious thought to give it life.

I gripped the blankets to my chest as if they were the only thing keeping me on this earth.

Someone pounded on my door, shaking the wood, the chair still wedged beneath trembling with the force of it.

"Emma Grace!" Percy shouted.

Percy. My knight in shining armor. I pulled myself together, snatching my robe and flinging it around my shoulders.

"Lady Hastings?" another guest called.

"Emma Grace, are you hurt?" Andrew's voice.

I stumbled on a rug before reaching the door. With shaking fingers, I removed the satin seated chair and tossed it aside like an old glove. Wrenching the deadbolt back, I flung open the door.

Percy and Andrew charged into the room, Mrs. Wentworth in her night cap and a long braid over her shoulder peering in. The others were gathering in the hall behind, presumably to find the cause of all the ruckus.

"Has someone else been offed?" Mr. Campbell asked.

I detested the man.

"Emma Grace, whatever is the matter?" Percy asked.

Andrew said nothing, his eyes searching my person.

My breath was coming in tight gasps, and I pointed shakily to the offending flower. I cinched my robe tighter about my neck as I felt the chill of the horrifying discovery all over.

The murderer could have left the rose.

Someone had been in my room. After the door had been bolted and barred.

I fisted my fingers to keep them from trembling.

"What? What is it?" Percy asked again. He gripped my shoulders, staring into my eyes. His were cupped with deep shadows, his pallor gray. His shirt was untucked and unbuttoned, exposing a sizeable V of his muscled chest.

"The rose," I gasped out. My teeth chattered.

"Here." Andrew took off his jacket and draped it over my shoulders.

Immediately I was surrounded by Andrew's mint and fresh soap smell.

"The rose," I said again, steadier this time. "It was not there last night."

"Did you bar your door?" Andrew asked, eyes sharp as he looked me over once more before flitting his gaze to the door and back to the rose. My fuddled mind absently registered that Andrew was fully dressed while the rest of us were still in our night clothes.

I nodded. "I did. The deadbolt was locked, and the chair wedged securely," I confirmed.

Andrew squared his jaw.

"Emma Grace, surely the rose was there, you just don't remember it?" Percy asked, brows drawn.

I shook my head. "No. There was no rose on the table last night." My cheeks flamed as I realized my scratching of suspects by the poem stanzas was likely still visible under the vase.

"Perhaps you wandered in your sleep, found it in some other corner of your room, and put it there yourself?" Mr. Angus offered, having come through the door.

Mrs. Wentworth huffed a breath, seemingly irritated with the whole affair.

"I assure you; it is not my imagination. *There was no rose or vase in this room last night*," I said icily. I did not appreciate my horror attributed merely to womanly hysterics.

"Emma Grace, surely. Yesterday was horrendous. What Mr. Angus says makes sense. It would be perfectly rational for you to move the flower without remembering you did so," Percy said with a gentle hand to my upper arm. His eyes were yet troubled. I wasn't sure if it was due to the rose or my obvious distress.

Indignation flared beneath my skin.

"She said she did not," came Andrew's curt reply. I narrowed my eyes at him. While part of me did appreciate his believing me—especially after my confessing last night that I wasn't sure if I thought him a killer or not—I didn't need him interfering with my relationship with Percy. In any way. After my disturbing conclusion last night that I was likely the one whose innocence was lost, I didn't want Andrew and Percy within twenty feet of each other.

"And I suppose you are an expert on Lady Hasting's mental status?" Percy asked, sarcasm heavy in his tone.

Andrew glanced between us, at Percy's hand on my arm. I swallowed an acerbic response to Percy's commentary on my psyche.

"Obviously not," Andrew said, devoid of emotion.

Percy's nostril's flared and his fingers tightened ever so slightly against my bicep.

"The point is that *someone else* was in this room last night. And they did not come through that door." Andrew glanced around the room again as if willing new evidence to submit itself to his perusal.

"Women get hysterical at the silliest things," Lord Villiers mumbled.

Red splotched the edges of my vision and sharpened my tongue. "I suppose it would be a matter of no consequence had a possible murderer slipped unheard and unseen into your room last night and left a calling card?"

Lord Villiers had the grace to tug at the collar of his night shirt, his bare toes curling against the carpet.

"Where's Leonard? He'd know how a chap could sneak into a room here," Lord Asquith said. He leaned against the wall, eyes completely blood shot and face screwed up against the light.

"That's right—where are he and Mrs. Leonard?" Lady Algernon repeated.

"I could have sworn I overheard his voice saying something about keeping on schedule in the wee hours this morning," Lady Fulbright offered.

"Where did you hear him?" Mr. Campbell asked.

"From my bed," Lady Fulbright said with a dark glare in his direction. "I was awakened by a thumping noise, and thought I heard his voice mumbling about keeping on schedule. He's staff." She shrugged. "I thought nothing of it, assuming he was readying breakfast or some such chore. I rolled over and went back to sleep, though I find none of those details your concern," she said primly.

Mr. Angus snorted, earning him black looks from Lady Fulbright and Lord Villiers. It reinforced my deduction that they were having an affair with each other.

"Let's find them." Percy's tone was resigned. "Everyone get dressed and assemble at the end of the hallway. We'll go down the stairs together." Percy took charge, motioning with his hand to shoo everyone from the room before rubbing the heel of one hand against his right eye.

I cringed at the thought of being alone in my chambers—they were no longer a safe haven but felt like the scene of a new crime—a crime in which my security had been stolen.

"Would you like me to wait just outside the door?" Andrew's soft words tickled the hairs beside my ear.

I glanced at Percy. He was preoccupied with something Mr. Campbell had said to him and hadn't heard Andrew's question. I bit my lip.

"Darling?" Percy turned to me, yanking my attention from Andrew. "I'm just going to get dressed. I'll collect you immediately after." He tweaked my chin and herded the others toward the door.

I nodded minutely at Andrew. He tipped his head, letting me know my request had been acknowledged.

"Mr. Harrigan, if you please," Percy snapped. "I'd take it kindly if you did not let your eyes linger on my intended, particularly in her current state." *Of undress* was implied.

I gasped. *Intended*? Andrew lifted an eyebrow.

"My apologies, I did not realize." Andrew's voice was flat, and he did not look back at me as the two men left my room and shut the door behind them.

Not even so much as a by your leave from Percy after such a declaration.

Time enough to dwell on that later.

I whirled around, searching every nook and crevice of my room. Nothing. The fire was down to ashes. No servant had stirred them back to life. I gripped Andrew's jacket tighter about my shoulders. The scent of him was still a comfort as my eyes locked once more on the little table by the fireplace. Someone had taken the trouble to enter my sanctuary and leave me a red rose.

Red as fresh blood.

My finger stroked over the thin white line still visible on my finger where the original Mistlethwaite envelope had cut me.

CHAPTER TEN

Andrew and Percy were fixed in a deadlock, staring holes into each other's foreheads when I opened my door fifteen minutes later.

My hand slid to the lowest button on my brown velveteen jacket, just below my belly button where strange things flapped and slithered inside.

I cleared my throat. "Your coat, Mr. Harrigan. Thank you for its use." I handed him the black garment.

"And why do you have his coat?" Percy asked, eyes growing large as he seemed to only just notice my apparent association with Andrew as I held his jacket.

"She was shivering this morning, so I lent it to her," Andrew said mildly, flipping it over his arm casually. As he did, I noted a dark reddish-brown stain upon the cuff of his shirt.

It was shockingly like a blood spatter.

Nausea churned in my gut.

"First you lend her your jacket, then I find you lying in wait outside her door," Percy accused.

"I'd hardly say I was lying in wait," Andrew deadpanned.

"Then what would you call it, lurking outside her *bedroom*?" Percy's volume raised and I wanted to wither into the watered silk wall covering.

Mrs. Wentworth stepped closer like a vulture ready to pounce upon an unexpected meal. Lady Algernon finished locking her door, then stood, watching us. The commotion drew the rest of the men from their rooms as well.

"While you were pomading yourself up like a peacock, I was standing guard to ensure Lady Hastings's safety. There is obviously another way into her chambers, and I did not wish anything sinister to befall her. It is easier to rush to someone's rescue from three feet away than it is from thirty feet away down the corridor."

Sparks were practically jumping between the two of them. Though as I watched the argument unfolding, I did note the differences between the two men. Percy was a few inches taller, his hair pomaded to perfection, his clothes clean and pressed. Andrew's hair was mussed—rather attractively—over his forehead, his clothes rumpled, and as I looked closer, the same shirt he'd had on last night. The pants were different though no less rumpled—as if he'd slept in them, and the jacket he'd put over my shoulders was a day coat, not his tails from last night's dinner. There was a light covering of stubble over Andrew's jaw. Percy had shaved.

And Andrew had a bloodstain on his cuff.

My heart accelerated and my mouth dried.

"Ooh, entertainment before breakfast," Mr. Campbell sniped. Lord Asquith snorted a laugh. I glared at them both, wishing for bolts of lightning to fly from my eyes.

"Stop this ridiculous display and let's go find the Leonards," Lord Villiers said.

Lady Fulbright exited her room, locked it, and gingerly touched the lace of the high neck of her dress, tugging it up toward her jaw.

"Stay away from Lady Hastings." Percy growled the words so low I doubted anyone but the three of us heard them.

I blinked, incredulous at this uncharacteristic show of possession. Percy had never acted in anything other than a gallant fashion toward me, and a part of my brain told me I ought to be flattered at such attentions, but for the moment, they rankled. I didn't appreciate feeling like a pawn in some unseen game of chess. Tension laced the air.

Before I could comment, Percy grabbed my hand and tucked it into the crook of his elbow and marched us toward the stairs.

I glanced back at Andrew, but his face was a stony mask of indifference.

The Leonards were not in the kitchen. They were not in the dining room. They were not in their shared bedroom in the servants' quarters. There was no breakfast cooking, though there were baskets of scones and pastry on the sideboard in the dining room. But no eggs, no sausage, no bacon, no tea...nothing fresh. Not even clotted cream or jam.

"They've blasted flew the coop!" Mr. Campbell complained.

"And how could they leave?" Mr. Angus countered. He gestured to the windows of the dining room where muted white light was all that showed between the blinding force of the blizzard still moaning against the manor.

"Then where are they?" Lady Algernon asked. Her gaze skittered around like a frantic mouse, landing on Mr. Campbell, holding a moment, then scurrying away.

No one answered.

If they hadn't quit the manor, and they weren't where they ought or answering our summons, given last night's events, would it be logical to assume they were...

Deceased?

Surely, they were merely some place in this huge house where they could not hear our calls. Bad form to disappear on the guests they'd been hired to look after, but from their perspective, I suppose their benefactor had just been murdered. They were unlikely to get paid. Unless the pair of them were the ones that killed Lord Barclay. That would give them a whole different reason to hide.

"I'm going nowhere until I've eaten something," complained Lord Asquith. He traipsed to the sideboard and loaded a plate with two scones and three pastries. And then proceeded to fill a tea cup full of brandy from the decanter left from last night.

"Steady on, man," Mr. Angus blurted.

Lord Asquith gave a mocking half salute with his mug of spirits then downed three enormous gulps of it. He smacked his lips and sat down at the table, slinging one leg over the arm of the chair.

"Do, make yourself comfortable," Mr. Campbell retorted.

"Isn't anyone worried that we haven't found the Leonards?" I asked. Anxiety gnawed like my grumbling belly.

"Yes," Percy said at the same time Andrew answered, "Of course."

Mrs. Wentworth primly dabbed at her lips, watching Andrew and Percy as they glared at each other.

"If they're already dead, they'll still be dead yet after breaking fast," Mr. Campbell said as he grabbed a plate.

Lady Algernon gasped in horror at his blunt words.

"We don't know for certain they *are* dead," Percy interjected.

"Don't you think the decent thing to do would be to ensure that they aren't lying injured somewhere?" Andrew asked, his disdain evident in the way his brown gaze narrowed.

"Yes, of course," Lady Fulbright said. She tugged the collar of her dress higher.

"Don't let us keep you," Lord Asquith said around a mouthful of flaky pastry.

"Heathen," Mrs. Wentworth aimed at the young lord as he sprawled, drank his brandy, and showered his vest with crumbs.

"Let's go search," Andrew said softly.

I nodded, and to my surprise, so did Percy. I half expected him to rebel at the suggestion simply because it came from my former fiancé. My empty stomach twisted in knots. I could not let Andrew tell Percy that he'd kissed me. I didn't think he would, but we were all under a lot of pressure, and pressure sometimes made people crack. This was one fissure I couldn't afford on the off chance that Percy or his family would find it grounds to refuse me a marriage proposal. My own future and that of my family were at stake if I did not marry well—which meant my marrying the young Lord Fairfax. My family was depending on me. I could not let them down.

"Emma Grace, darling, stay here. Eat something. You must be famished. This could be...grisly," Percy said on a hard swallow. Gray shadows leeched the color from his blue eyes. The strain of events must be riding him harder than he was admitting. Poor man. It was still gallant of him to face things head on. But as his words settled on me, a chill whipped up my spine. I glanced at the other guests, then back to Percy and Andrew.

I did not know the other guests, what they were capable of, and I wasn't entirely certain Andrew hadn't had something to do with Lord Barclay's demise, but what I did know was that of the people assembled, I trusted Andrew Harrigan and Percy Crofton more.

Doubts and second guesses were whirling through me faster than the snow thrashing outside. But given the choice of Andrew or Percy over the other guests? I thought I still trusted both men with my safety, even if I wasn't entirely certain that Andrew was innocent.

"No." I shook my head, adamant in my choice. "I'll go with you."

Percy's jaw ticked while Andrew's shoulders relaxed a fraction. "Safety in numbers," Andrew said.

"Actually," Mr. Angus said, "it mightn't be a bad idea to go in groups of three to search for the Leonards. Assuming the murderer is among us, going in groups of three should offer some protection."

"Surely the Leonards are merely on some errand in a far corner of the house," Lady Algernon said. Her fingers trembled where she clutched them into her shawl.

"At any rate, we need to find them," Lady Fulbright inserted.

"Agreed. But let's not have you in a group with Lord Villiers, just in case the two of you teamed up to do in Lord Barclay over your secret tryst," Mrs. Wentworth spat with venom.

Lord Villiers spluttered with indignation while Lady Fulbright blushed as red as the rose left in my room.

Lord Asquith squished a burp behind his lips. "Oh, come off it, old man. What's the upset over an affair? Gentlemen of the aristocracy do it all the time. As long as discretion is the order of the day, what's the bother?" Lord Asquith took a slurp of his brandy and waved his hand in the air as if dismissing the pair of them.

Dread bloomed in my chest. He wasn't incorrect. And it wasn't a well-known affair, or I'd likely have heard of it in my own social circles. Gossip spread quicker than a port wine stain on white lace, so they must have been discreet. If that was truly the case, not many would bat an eye at it. But then how had Lord Barclay discovered their spouse-fleecing? The nausea churned harder, spreading tentacles of trepidation throughout my shoulder blades.

Mr. Angus tapped his lower lip, his cheap black suit shifted, revealing his wrist as he did. "Unless Lord Villiers has an American heiress as a wife."

Lord Villiers paled, his complexion going from tomato red to ashy gray in an instant.

Mr. Angus continued. "An American heiress who had a prenuptial agreement that allowed her to seek a divorce and keep any money and inheritance she brought with her to the marriage upon her husband's infidelity."

Lord Villiers was struck silent. Lady Fulbright wrung her hands, glancing frantically between William Angus and her lover.

"Say something, Raymond." She hissed the words on a sob.

"Who are you?" Lord Villiers asked Mr. Angus.

"William Angus. No lord or sir attached. Common as common gets."

Another line of the poem completed then.

"The Leonards?" I broke in before another explosion of verbal assaulting could start.

CHAPTER ELEVEN

In the end, I went to check the east wing with Percy and Andrew—because I trusted them most, and because I wanted to ensure my own secrets were safe. I was relatively certain Andrew was the only other soul who knew we'd kissed, save Lord Barclay, but he had hopefully taken my secret to his untimely grave. Lord Villiers grouped with Mrs. Wentworth, Lady Algernon, and William Angus to check the west wing of the house while Lady Fulbright stayed in the dining room with Mr. Campbell and Lord Asquith. It felt like an uneasy truce for the moment while we searched for the missing staff.

The east wing of the house was familiar territory as it held the library, the great hall, the room where we'd found Lord Barclay—I shivered—as well as the study where his corpse lay.

"Emma Grace, are you certain you won't stay in the dining room? I hate for you to be exposed to such cruelties as this. If only I could spirit you away from all of this," Percy bemoaned as we neared the ballroom.

I fidgeted with the bottom button of my jacket. The smooth grain of my wine-colored skirt trimmed in matching velveteen swished against the marble floor. It was a comforting sound amidst the frightening echoes our footfalls made in the monolithic space otherwise devoid of life.

"I am certain, though I thank you for your concern," I said. "I do not wish to be..." How could I say it delicately?

"Alone with the two Cretins stuffing their faces?" Andrew supplied, and I snorted an unladylike titter before I could keep it in.

I flashed him a grateful smile before Percy turned and glared at him. I tempered my expression, though Andrew's words had lightened the moment for me considerably.

"Something like that," I conceded.

Percy's lips twitched, though in smile or frown, I couldn't quite tell.

We searched the great hall, the salon, the gallery where I'd walked alone in darkness the night before. We scoured all the rooms leading up to the study. Once we reached the door, I hesitated.

"We must check to be thorough," Andrew said, his fingers brushing my elbow. Tingles rushed from my scalp to my toes.

"Stay here. Don't look. It may remind you of too much unpleasantness from last night," Percy said. Concern drew his brows together as he glanced at me.

I swallowed thickly and nodded, bracing my shoulders against the wall beside the door. Andrew nodded to me once then Percy opened the door. My hand flew to my mouth, and I bit down on my fist as emotions rose within me, fighting to escape. Refusing to close my eyes, I kept them glued to the long hallway we'd just come down while the men made a quick search of the room.

"All as it was," Andrew said as he exited, clearing his throat.

"Ghastly business." Percy shut the door, his face a shade paler than it had been going in.

"There's only the library left, I suppose," I said, eager to be done with our macabre chore, and desperately hoping we did not find Mr. or Mrs. Leonard.

At least not in a deadened state. I was very much in favor of finding them alive.

We traversed the short corridor to the library. Percy turned the knob and swung open the door. The mustiness of books permeated into the hallway, but it was the immediate straightening of Percy's shoulders that warned me of the sinister things worse than badly written books lurking in the room.

Andrew elbowed Percy out of the way, swearing softly.

"Is it bad?" I asked, both curious and ill at the gruesome thoughts stampeding through my brain.

"It—" Andrew cleared his throat.

"It's Mrs. Leonard," Percy rasped.

Curiosity overcame my good judgement, and I peeked through the valley made between the two men's shoulders.

A low moan escaped my lips.

"Emma Grace, please turn away," Percy pleaded.

"It's not that," I stammered, even though it was. But her dead body slumped over a reading couch wasn't the worst part. It was the black silk shawl wound round her throat. "That's my shawl."

CHAPTER TWELVE

"It's what?" Percy's eyebrows hiked to his carefully pomaded hairline.

"Emma Grace?" Andrew said, nearly as aghast as Percy.

I shook my head as the world spun and a loud whirring began behind my ears. "I lost it— sometime last night. I meant to go and retrieve it, but then, well, with Lord Barclay. But..." I shrugged helplessly, nearly undone that an article of my clothing, something from my own person, had been used to cruelly strangle Mrs. Leonard and snuff out her life.

Her lips were open, tinged in blue, her face bloated and shadowed deep purple along her jaw line. I was suddenly glad I'd not eaten anything as my stomach twisted and flipped, nausea causing me to take shallow inhales through my mouth.

"We must retrieve it before the others find out," Percy said, sliding a hand through his pomaded hair and ruffling the strands out of place.

"What exactly are you retrieving?" Mr. Campbell asked, eyes glittering, hands shoved into his pockets as he sauntered up.

We'd been so engrossed in the death of poor Mrs. Leonard that none of us had heard Mr. Campbell sneaking up behind us. He wore soft leather-soled house shoes with his morning coat. The hairs on the back of my neck prickled as I took in his cat-that-caught-the-canary expression.

Andrew edged in front of me as Percy gripped my elbow.

"I think you'd better let me through to have a look," Mr. Campbell said, wedging his way through the knot of us clustered around the door.

He stopped a few paces inside the room and whistled. "That's a doozy. Reckon that's your black wrap, too, isn't it?" He glanced back at me, accusation thick in the arch of his brow and in his tone.

"She lost it last night," Percy offered weakly. "It doesn't mean she had anything to do with—with this." He gestured to the dead woman.

"Where are Lord Asquith and Lady Fulbright?" Andrew asked.

Mr. Campbell shrugged, bending to get a closer look at Mrs. Leonard's black silk wrapped neck. "Last I saw, they were in the dining room. That young Asquith, he can toss back the liquor. Francis Fulbright is just another rich man's wife having her bread and butter with someone else."

His dispassionate and casual reference to...married things...sent blood rushing to my face in mortification. Notably in front of Andrew and Percy.

"We agreed we'd stay in our groups," Andrew insisted, crossing his arms over his wide chest. Absently, I noticed—with an unavoidable degree of appreciation—how the jacket pulled tight over his shoulders and biceps.

Mr. Campbell straightened. "No. *You* agreed we'd stay in our groups. I never agreed to such balderdash."

"Help! Come quick!" someone shouted from far away down the hallway. In a collective rush, the four of us dashed from the room, Percy and Mr. Campbell getting slightly ahead, Andrew and I bringing up the rear.

Wretched skirts. Wretcheder corset.

Neither were made for quick movement, nor for running pell-mell down the old corridors of Mistlethwaite Manor.

We rounded the bend and tumbled as a group into the grand foyer where we'd first gained admittance to the house. The beautiful marble stairs twisted themselves up, white and elegant like the long neck of a fashionable woman.

"What's all the rush?" Percy asked, chest heaving.

I braced myself against a pillar, trying to catch my breath against the laced stays of my undergarments. I'd have left them off entirely if I'd thought I'd be dashing about like a mad woman. On that thought, perhaps it wouldn't be completely unwarranted to remove them at my earliest opportunity. The thought of entering my violated chambers again, even to preserve my constricted lungs, filled me with dread.

"There." Lady Algernon pointed a shaking finger to the hidden door concealed to perfection beneath the stairwell. Except that the latch hadn't caught, and a black crack stood in sharp relief against the rest of the white paint. A puddle of dark blood oozed beneath the door.

I thought I might be ill.

"Take breaths. You don't have to look." Andrew's fingers ghosted over my arm as his soft words floated over me. He met my gaze for an instant before inching forward toward the door.

"What's the hullabaloo?" Lord Asquith asked as he stepped unsteadily to the top of the staircase.

"Look down, you sozzled half-wit," Lord Villiers snapped. "Where's Francis?"

"No point in hiding it now, is there, my lord?" Mr. Campbell shot the older man a saucy grin that bordered on predatory.

Lord Asquith moaned before Lord Villiers could respond to the insult. The younger man clutched his head and stared at the pool of congealing blood.

Lady Fulbright appeared behind Lord Asquith, shrieking when she saw what held us all spellbound.

"We must open it," Mr. Angus said.

"Agreed," Andrew answered. "We're all here save the Leonards." His Adam's apple bobbed.

"Where is Mrs. Leonard? Did you find her?" Mrs. Wentworth asked, holding a delicate lace hankie to her nose. She cast about, as if only just noticing her absence.

"She won't be missing her husband anytime soon," Mr. Campbell supplied.

I held my breath, waiting for him to casually drop the murder weapon—my unintentional involvement—into the conversation.

"She what?" Mrs. Wentworth's eyes widened.

"Saints preserve us," Lady Algernon muttered.

"Well don't just stand there gawking. Open it," Lord Villiers demanded.

Andrew shot the man a withering glare then looked to Mr. Angus. He nodded. Andrew glanced back once at me then gripped the door, careful to avoid the puddle.

"Emma Grace, why are you looking?" Percy asked, a deep urgency in his voice. He stood in front of me, expression anguished, blocking my view of the vile thing we'd surely find behind the white door.

"Percy, stop. I *need* to see." Some dark part of me required my curiosity be sated. I needed to know the evil we faced. Shoving aside Percy's bulk, I poked my head out and bit my tongue hard enough it bled.

The puddle of blood stretching under the door was slight in comparison to the pool of blood inside the hidden closet space. Slumped over a work bench, Mr. Leonard's corpse could have been taking a rest but for the massive caved in place where the back of his skull should have been. And his brains spattered about. Bile rose in the back of my throat.

Lady Algernon screamed, and Lady Fulbright swooned, tipping into Lord Asquith who was still rooted to his place, staring on in horror.

"Francis!" Lord Villiers legged it up the staircase, cradling the woman in his arms before she could tumble down the expanse of white marble.

"I can't breathe," I whispered, suddenly feeling like everything was too tight—tight like a vice around my throat.

"Keep breathing." The voice came to my ears as if under water. "In and out. Breathe with me."

"Shove off," Percy said irritably.

Black dotted my vision, and my feet were unsteady.

"You're safe right now, Emma Grace." I latched onto that voice—somehow both familiar and far away.

"Of course, she's safe. I'm right here with her," Percy said. His hands caressed my shoulders.

Shaking my head, I blinked until my eyes focused. Andrew stood next to Percy. Neither of them appeared pleased with the other. Concern for my future itched at me, but my most pressing concern was removing my corset. I needed oxygen.

"I see why you prefer strangulation. Sight of blood does you in, eh?" Mr. Campbell fixed me with an oily grin.

All the living eyes in the room suddenly riveted on me.

CHAPTER THIRTEEN

I fought to maintain my hold on reality. I would not swoon.

"She what?" Mr. Angus said.

"Oh, didn't anyone mention? Mrs. Leonard was strangled to death with Lady Hasting's evening shawl." Mr. Campbell examined his fingernails.

"She has killed no one," Percy said.

Andrew crossed his arms, stepping fully in front of me.

"Of course, I haven't killed anyone," I rasped, mouth dry as cotton.

"You want to explain your shawl wrapped around Mrs. Leonard's neck?" Mr. Campbell asked.

Lady Fulbright whimpered and hobbled from Mr. Villiers's side to lean her head against a marble pillar. Her hand cupped around her throat as if in sympathy with Mrs. Leonard's fate. Dramatic altogether.

"Lady Hastings lost it in the fray of things last night, isn't that right, darling?" Percy said, menace edging his voice.

"I did. I misplaced it last night...sometime after dinner. I meant to retrieve it later but forgot about it entirely once Lord Barclay was discovered." My voice was scratchy. I needed water. And to loosen my laces.

"Awfully convenient," Lord Asquith said. He'd toddled down the stairs and now stood with the rest, all gathered around me in a half circle, Andrew and Percy flanking me. At least I still had their support.

"What did you have against Mrs. Leonard?" Mr. Angus asked.

"Nothing!" I cried. Sweat broke out along my hairline despite the chill in the cavernous room.

"Wicked child!" Mrs. Wentworth disparaged.

"Right! Perhaps she went out to strangle the staff last night, and then left the rose in her room herself to deflect attention!" Lord Villiers said.

"How could you?" Lady Algernon whispered.

Hateful words spewed from the guests, falling out on top of each other.

"Stop!" Andrew roared—loud enough my bones trembled with the echo of his words. "Stop," he repeated firmly. "Let us look at the facts. Even if Lady Hastings had been inclined to do away with

Mrs. Leonard, why would she have used her own evening wrap? Has anyone stopped to consider whether or not Lady Hastings even has the strength to strangle another? Mrs. Leonard was taller and larger than Lady Hastings. And then let us turn our attention to Mr. Leonard. Who among you thinks a woman as delicate as Lady Hastings has the heft to club a man in the back of the head with enough force to crush his skull?"

Silence reigned the room, and I swallowed any pride at the attention brought to my apparent lack of strength, true as it was.

"Mr. Harrigan is right," Percy intoned. His steely gaze landed on each guest. "It seems it would make the most sense that a pair of murderers is at work. Someone to lure, someone to kill. Lady Hastings is part of no such evil pairing."

Lord Villiers's eyes narrowed as several guests glanced to him and Lady Fulbright. "Or a singular murderer who killed first one in one wing of the house, then killed the other after in quick succession. Someone of strength." The older man glared at Percy, then Andrew, then Mr. Angus, Mr. Campbell, and Lord Asquith in succession.

I was suddenly not so offended at my absence of heft.

"What secrets do you hide, gentlemen?" Mr. Angus said. His posture was taut, keeping close watch on everything, his dark eyes assessing.

I swallowed and glanced at the door, wishing desperately that I could fling it open and leave this place forever, never looking back. My heart stopped as I noticed a tiny smudge of brownish red beneath the doorknob. A single drip of dried blood crusted on the marble directly beneath.

"Look, we're getting nowhere arguing in this freezing vestibule. Perhaps we could argue somewhere warmer. Preferably with a snifter of Scotch." Lord Asquith's eyes were still glassy, though for once, I appreciated his comments. I was all but shivering.

"I'd like to visit my room first," I gasped.

"What is it, Emma Grace?" Percy asked, his concerned gaze flying over me.

"I..." I cleared my throat. "I need to attend to a matter of my garment."

"Hiding blood evidence, no doubt," Mr. Campbell muttered.

"Have one of the ladies come with me and watch, if you're that concerned," I snapped. I knew I had no blood upon my person—unlike Andrew. I bit the inside of my cheek. I needed to speak with him. But there was no reason I couldn't turn some of this wretched situation to my own advantage. By taking someone else with me into my room, at least I wouldn't have to be alone in the event someone came back to drop me more sinister gifts. Or find me with greater ill intent.

CHAPTER FOURTEEN

With much bickering, accusations, and general distrust, the group of us eventually made it up the steps to the third floor. My corset pressed against me painfully, driving my anxiety higher than it already was.

"Be quick," Mr. Campbell grumped. I glared at him.

"Patience," Percy chided him.

Andrew met my gaze, his offering silent support. I desperately needed to ask him about the blood on his shirt, because past feelings were surely clouding my judgment where he was concerned. Some of the old anger and hurt still flared when I looked at him, but I also found myself desiring his protection and his company—the easy comradery we once held.

And those were the thoughts I must banish, for they'd tarnish my future with Percy as surely as my scarf had been the instrument of murder for Mrs. Leonard.

Clenching my fingers into a fist lest they tremble in front of everyone assembled, I willed them to work properly and dug my room key from my reticule.

"Let us go in," Mrs. Wentworth said in a huff.

I cringed, wishing she had not been appointed with Lady Algernon to be the ones who would come with me into my rooms, but I had no other options save Lady Fulbright, and I liked her no more than I liked Mrs. Wentworth.

Clearing my throat, I shut the door behind us. "Thank you for coming with me," I said, attempting politeness.

"Come, come. We haven't all day," Mrs. Wentworth snipped.

I turned and rolled my eyes. We had nothing *but* time. Time and a murderer on the loose. We could not leave until the storm let up, and it didn't appear to be running out of steam. As if to mock me, a *thunk* of ice blasted against the glass pane. My shoulders twitched.

"If you'll just excuse me, I'll change."

"What do you think you're doing, going behind that dressing screen?" Mrs. Wentworth's sharp words bit at my shoulders, and I turned back to face the older women.

"I meant to change, as I said."

"Not back there you won't. We cannot see if you've hidden away a knife or some other horrific sin or stain of your misdeeds. You'll change here where we can observe your debauchery and your villainy."

Anger lashed beneath my skin. The gall of this woman!

"Margaret, she's just a girl. And it *was* her room that was broken into," Lady Algernon offered.

"Quiet, Rose!" Mrs. Wentworth turned the full blast of her glacial stare on Lady Algernon. The slighter woman seemed to shrivel beneath her gaze.

Refusing to let her bitter words affect me any more than they already had, I unbuttoned the velvet-covered buttons on my jacket. Might as well get the awkwardness over with. It's not as if I didn't have a lady's maid who frequently saw my nakedness to help me dress and undress. But I was certain my lady's maid wasn't a murderess. I wasn't convinced such could be said for my current companions.

I shivered as I draped my jacket over the chair. My shirt sleeves were thin, fine cotton. Actually, the entire manor was frigid with no staff to keep the fires stoked. I realized the coals in my own hearth had all but gone out. It would likely be cold the remainder of my time in this wretched place. Crossing the room to my trunk, I pulled out the most evocative piece of clothing I owned. It had been gifted to me in private by an American heiress friend who had ties to the dress reform movement. My mother did not know of its existence. Despite the garment's scandalous nature, it was also the most functional vestment in my trousseau. I went nowhere without it, and today, I was most glad of it.

Glancing at the other two women in my periphery, I turned my back to them and quickly undid the pins on my blouse and let my skirt drop to the floor. My layers of petticoats soon followed.

"Whatever are you doing?" Mrs. Wentworth complained.

"Taking care that I don't catch a chill." And making sure I would be able to run for my life, should the need arise. I couldn't do that in a corset and twelve layers of petticoats.

Despite my earlier thoughts of being naked in front of my ladies' maid, it was quite another to be unclothed to my skin in front of these judgmental crows. Clenching my teeth against the embarrassment scorching my chest, I undid the laces of my corset, breathing deeply as the constricting metal bands were lifted from my skin.

"Blasphemy. What sort of sinful creature are you to behave so provocatively? Do up your laces at once!" Mrs. Wentworth's voice held every possible measure of censure and disdain. She went so far as to take a step toward me, as if she meant to do my laces back up herself.

I stepped away. "Brace yourself, Mrs. Wentworth," I said, fortifying myself, as I slipped out of my chemise and drawers, leaving my bare body to their full examination.

Mrs. Wentworth sucked in a horrified breath and let a most unladylike oath drop from her lips. I didn't dare turn my front to them, but quickly as I could, stepped into my *chemiloon*—a one-piece under garment. If I'd been a man, I'd have called it my union suit or my long Johns. The soft flannel hugged my skin in warmth as I did up the buttons. I forwent the layers of petticoats, instead slipping my chemise back on, one petticoat, and tied on only my bustle so my skirts wouldn't drag the ground over much. It didn't take me long to finish pinning my shirt in place and buttoning up my wool-lined velveteen jacket overall. I was still cool, but as my last shawl had ended up a murder weapon, I wasn't sure I should take my chances. Fear that another article in my possession might be used to harm another once more, I forwent the extra wrap.

At last, I turned back to face the women. Mrs. Wentworth sneered in disapproval. "Clearly, you are either lowborn or a woman of loose morals. Either way, I want nothing to do with you and your sins." She turned her nose up and marched herself out the door, leaving it cracked in her wake.

"Have you figured out anyone else?" Lady Algernon asked.

I whirled to find her hunched over my scribbles next to Lord Barclay's poem. Blood rushed to my cheeks. "Oh, um, no. I haven't."

"Such a wretched affair. Horace...he wasn't always bad. But mostly he is."

"Lady Algernon?" Her words made no sense. "Mostly he is what?"

"Bad." She sighed. "But not always. Not my Horace." Her words were little more than a mumble, and I wasn't certain I heard her correctly. Her Horace?

"Did you share a history with Lord Barclay?" Prickles skittered over my scalp. Did Lady Algernon have the capacity to murder? To drive a knife into Horace Barclay's back? Had he wronged her—or had he merely discovered something she wished to keep secret?

She smiled—a grim thing that froze the blood in my veins.

"Oh, a history, yes, yes. It was Algy that saved me, but then I saved myself." She turned manic eyes on me, and a shot of adrenaline raced to my extremities. "Pushed him down the stairs, I did. Served him right. Horace was bad, but Algy was cruel. None for me. None for me." She shook her head and warning bells clanged in my head. "I know. I know who killed my Horace."

"Who?" I hardly breathed the word.

She gave me another toothy grin that was anything but reassuring. "I heard them. Saw the shadows. I never went to the kitchens. I wanted to stay and talk with Horace, but then I saw the other one."

"Who? What did you see?" I frantically pushed her to say the words.

She cackled. "Oh, my dear, I know where the prize is." Her smile turned slightly sinister, and those warning bells turned into gongs of alarm.

"Emma Grace, are you finished?" Percy called through the door. Assuring that Lady Algernon stayed within my periphery, I glanced at the door. Mrs. Wentworth had exited without us, leaving the door cracked. As much as I wanted answers, I wanted to be alive after I had them. And the way Lady Algernon was gripping the metal-tipped quill did not in any way endear her to me.

"Yes! Yes, I'm finished." The words came out an octave higher than I meant them to. Rushing to the door, I flung it back and stepped out. Andrew still waited on one side while Percy stood on the other. Mr. Campbell looked utterly bored while Mr. Angus fidgeted his fingers against the spine of a book, looking at the pages but seeming not to really see them. Lord Asquith took a pull from a flask.

"This is a woman of loose morals. I have no doubt that she is the one 'born on the wrong side of the sheets' *and* with her 'innocence lost.'"

"Mrs. Wentworth, truly, I envy those who have never met you." The words exploded from my lips as my anger boiled over. Mr. Angus snorted and looked up, surprised, from the book he was not reading.

"And just which line pertains to you?" Andrew asked the uppity woman. "Are you so willing to accuse others without confessing your own motivations for murder?" He still leaned against my door jamb, arms crossed casually, though from my vantage, I could see the tension lining his back. His fingers fisted beneath his elbow.

"Worthless, utterly foozled," Mr. Campbell said in a singsong voice.

Mrs. Wentworth narrowed her eyes at him.

"When was the last time Horace Barclay foozled you, Mrs. Wentworth?" Mr. Angus asked as he laid his book on an inlaid mother-of-pearl table by the wall.

"I do not answer to common trash."

"Perhaps not, but you may answer to a magistrate if any of your vitriol translated into action. I wouldn't put it past a shrew like you to commit murder to get what you wanted or to exact revenge." Mr. Angus's eyes were bright while twin spots of red stood out on Mrs. Wentworth's cheeks.

"Where are Lord Villiers and Lady Fulbright?" I asked, suddenly noting their absence. Dread clawed at me.

Lady Algernon stumbled, colliding into Percy's chest. "Oh, Lord Fairfax, what shall we do?" she crooned into Percy's face, a glint in her eyes. The stress of things must have addled her senses. The woman was unhinged.

"Search for them," Mr. Angus said.

Seizing the chance to speak to him while the others—namely Percy—were preoccupied, I tugged Andrew's sleeve before walking briskly toward the bedrooms to look for the missing guests. He followed, a silent shadow, both a comfort and torment at my back.

"Andrew, why is there blood on your cuff?" I whispered as we peered into one of the communal washrooms. A pink bar of soap rested on the ledge of the sink next to a tin of arsenic wafers advertised to be healthful to the skin.

"There is?" He sounded genuinely surprised. Glancing back, the others were all too busy searching along the hallway and the other rooms to notice the two of us. Andrew thrust his arms out, tugging his jacket sleeves back. The stain was there.

He frowned. "It must have happened last night when I moved Barclay's body."

"Not when you bludgeoned Mr. Leonard to death?" I whispered, lack of time making my words sharp and to the point.

Pain flashed across his features. "Emma Grace, do you sincerely think I would?"

"I don't want to." It was the truth. "But you had motive if the Leonards were in on Lord Barclay's duplicity in your family's finances, opportunity to bash his skull in, and the occasion to do it under the cover of night. Your clothes are rumpled like you've been wearing them too long, and you have blood on your shirt." I eyed his bicep, noting how snugly the material of his jacket lay over the muscle beneath. "And you have the strength to do it."

"I slept scarcely two hours last night because I stayed awake. There are many things wrong here at Mistlethwaite Manor. I have no intention of becoming one of them. I did not change into my night clothes, and yes, this is the same shirt I wore yesterday. I've sunk low enough in the opinion of the aristocracy that a wrinkled day-old shirt is hardly going to sink public opinion further."

I stared at him, his brown eyes so familiar. Looking into them, his expression was open. His eyes were tinged in red, and he did look tired, but there was an earnestness lingering there that I had dearly missed.

"Are you scared of me, Emma Grace? Do you think I'd hurt *you*?"

I searched his deep gaze once more—a soul I once thought I knew better than any other.

"No," I said, surprising us both.

"Good. Because I'd die before I'd let anything happen to you."

Including murder?

Suddenly Percy broke the moment. "What are the two of you doing here? Emma Grace, you must stay close to me at all times," Percy said as he threw Andrew a scathing look.

"Of course. I thought you were just behind us as we were searching." It wasn't a complete lie. I *knew* he was behind us. Far enough behind us he wouldn't hear me questioning Andrew.

Andrew smirked behind Percy's back, letting me know he was well aware of what I truly thought. I rolled my eyes at the insufferable man, took Percy's arm, and turned to go to the next room.

A scream rent the air and yet again, I found myself running down a long corridor. At least this time I could keep up and was still breathing normally when Percy, Andrew, and I reached the others clumped around Lord Villiers's chamber.

Lady Fulbright was perched on the bed, nearly hysterical, her clothing half on, lace neck of her dress unbuttoned and dangling open to expose ugly purple bruises at the base of her throat. Her shoes and one stocking were discarded on the floor, and her skirt was hanging askew enough that every one of us had a clear view of her leg up to her thigh.

Lord Villiers was not so hysterical. In fact, I doubted he'd ever have the chance to be so again. He lay face down on the carpet, the shattered remains of a white pottery vase in shards around him, embedded in his hair. Blood surrounded him. The bed was mussed— I clapped a hand over my mouth as I took in the sharp corner of the end table covered in blood and a little tuft of Lord Villiers's hair.

"H-he—he came after me," Lady Fulbright stammered. "I had to do it. He would have killed me!"

As nobody else was moving, I entered the room, skirting the body on the floor—truly, it was far less shocking to see a dead Lord Villiers than it had been to see a dead Lord Barclay, more so after witnessing both the Leonards deceased.

Taking care, as I wasn't completely certain Lady Fulbright was in her right mind, but knowing Percy and Andrew were just out of reach should she fly at me, I gently came to the woman's side.

"There, there, it's done now," I said softly as I adjusted her skirt so that it fell to cover her leg down to her ankle.

"No. You—you don't. Don't understand. I had to. I was in fear for my mortal life!" the woman wailed.

"How did your neck get injured?" I asked softly, conscious of the rest of the guests just inside the door and crowded outside.

Lady Fulbright shuddered a gasp, her hand flying to her throat, gaze almost unseeing at her dead lover. "I—we...Raymond liked—he liked to put his hands around my throat when we..." She drifted off, for which I was thankful. I didn't need any more details on their intimate trysts than I already knew. "And when Mrs. Leonard"—she rasped her name— "turned up strangled, I had this horrible thought—this weight of dread sitting on my chest. And when Raymond pulled me aside to, to indulge in some...convivial society, he put his hands at my neck, and he lost control. I swear he was going to kill me. I crushed the vase over him, and then he dropped off me, but he hit his head on the table on the way, then he fell to the floor."

She hiccoughed into the silence, and no one seemed to have words for what had just occurred.

"I cannot be in here with *him*!" Lady Fulbright shrieked. She leaped from the bed, knocking into my forehead in her mad dash to the exit. She plowed through those at the door, her leaving punctuated only by one more scream—though it wasn't hers.

The new commotion drew everyone from the doorway back into the hallway, leaving me alone in the room with dead Lord Villiers.

I swallowed and rubbed my aching forehead. The shock wasn't having the same effect on my system as it had earlier, but I still couldn't manage to tear my eyes from the little tuft of his hair and congealed blood on the corner of the end table.

"It seems to me that Lord Fairfax is generally unscathed here, and that you are rather attached to him. Tell me, why do you suppose that is?" Mr. Campbell sauntered back into the room, leering at me.

Where were Percy and Andrew? Fear and adrenaline dumped a toxic cocktail in my belly, whirling my anxiety up to new levels. I replied as evenly as I could. "If you'll recall, I've spent the morning dodging rumors set to ruin my character."

Mr. Campbell's icy gaze bore into me. "I think mayhap the two of you masterminded this whole affair in order to win the prize money. Then things got out of hand, you killed Barclay, and now the pair of you are tying up loose ends."

Breath froze in my lungs as he took a menacing step toward me. Then another. "I'd love to hear you scream," he said with a wicked grin.

Fear closed off my throat and I couldn't have made a squeak even if I'd been unfrozen enough to do so.

"Take one more step toward Lady Hastings and I'll put a bullet in your brain."

CHAPTER FIFTEEN

M r. Campbell whirled, fright widening his eyes as he found himself face to face with the gun Andrew pointed at his head.

"What, why, how do you have a gun?" he sputtered.

"Emma Grace, are you hurt?" Andrew asked.

"I am not hurt," I said, breathless and heart pounding painfully against my breastbone.

"Blast it all, why do you have a gun?" Mr. Angus blustered.

"I have a gun because I found it protruding from a suitcase ready to be carried upstairs last night before making my way to the dining room."

"You killed Lord Barclay!" Lord Asquith shouted.

"You'll note he was stabbed, not shot," Andrew countered, never once taking his eyes from Mr. Campbell.

"*You*! How? Give me the gun at once," Percy demanded, visibly shaken as he reentered the fray to find Andrew's hand gripped around the pistol.

"No, I don't think I will," Andrew said evenly.

"You can't go masquerading around with *that* firearm!" Mrs. Wentworth shrieked. Her eyes were wild with fear I'd never seen her exhibit.

"Lower it this instant! You might hit Emma Grace!" Spittle fairly flew from Percy's lips.

"I have uncommonly good aim," Andrew said. "Emma Grace, move along the edge of the bed then around the back of me to the door." The gun never wavered in his hand.

I did as he said, relief so potent my joints felt rubbery with it.

"Killing, yes; murder, no," Andrew whispered as I neared his person.

Before I could respond, Percy grabbed me, nearly crushing me to his chest as soon as I was in reach. But it wasn't Percy my eyes found. My gaze traced the straight set of Andrew's shoulders and the unwavering aim of the gun he pointed at Mr. Campbell.

"Oh, this is just bang up to the elephant," Lord Asquith said, his last word slurring.

"Give me back my gun!" Mrs. Wentworth screeched.

"*Your* gun?" Andrew turned his head enough to glance at the lady. Clearly, she was quite beside herself. If she'd had feathers her flapping about would have made her the perfect bird.

"Did you kill him? Lord Barclay?" Percy asked Mrs. Wentworth.

"If I'd had the opportunity, I would have used the gun and shot him straight through his wicked heart the way he forced my husband to kill himself with that very firearm!" With those jaw-dropping words, Mrs. Wentworth crumpled to the ground, sobs ripping from her throat. "Rose! Now Rose is gone, too!" She wailed in agony, an undignified heap on the carpet runner.

"Rose? What's happened to Lady Algernon?" I asked Percy, suppressing a shiver as I remembered her manic eyes. "Wait, I think she knows who the murderer is. She said she knew—said she saw in the shadows—"

"She's gone, Emma Grace," Percy said, his eyes haunted. "She tripped on her dress and fell down the stairs."

"Broke her neck." Lord Asquith made a cracking noise that made me wince.

"This house is cursed," Lady Fulbright muttered, sinking down next to Mrs. Wentworth.

I was inclined to agree.

CHAPTER SIXTEEN

L ady Algernon did indeed lay contorted at the bottom of the stairs. If not for the unnatural angle of her neck and her placement down a long flight of marble steps, she'd have looked peaceful. Maybe her tormented mind had finally found its rest.

Though I wished she'd confided in me who the murderer was first.

A chilling thought stole my breath. What if she'd been pushed? What if she hadn't tripped at all, but someone had helped her along with a subtle shove that sent her sprawling down the hard steps to her doom? Because they knew she was aware of their dark deeds?

I shook my head.

"Emma Grace, you've eaten nothing today. Surely, you must need sustenance," Percy said, his blue eyes concernedly sweeping my face. My heart did not go pitter-pat at his concern, though I wished it would.

I wasn't entirely certain I could eat anything, but I probably should try. Indeed, if I did need to make a run for any other reason—and that was a chief reason why I'd put on my *chemiloon* and removed my corset—it wouldn't do to get three feet then faint from hunger.

"You're right, of course," I conceded.

Gently taking my arm, Percy lead me away from the others toward the staircase at the opposite end of the hallway, away from Rose Algernon's corpse. He paused several paces and called over his shoulder, "Move the body. Put her to rest in her room."

"Where are you going?" Andrew asked, swiveling toward us.

"I'm taking poor Lady Hastings away from this. She's had no nourishment at all. All this stress cannot be good on her psyche."

Andrew's jaw ticked and he fastened his gaze on me. I nodded. I was safe with Percy. He'd practically declared his intentions last night, calling me his fiancé before bidding me goodnight. Percy would keep me safe. Percy had no blood on his cuff and hadn't been late to dinner last night either.

I must be terribly traumatized—the thought of becoming Mrs. Percival Crofton didn't bring an immediate smile to my lips. The thought of Andrew being the culprit beyond imagining, indeed, it was his arm I wished I was clinging to. Too much distress and no food. Surely, that was all it was.

"I'll come with you," Andrew said, my heart twinging with his words.

"There is no need. I shall take the utmost care of Lady Hastings," Percy insisted, his words icy.

"What about our agreement to go in threes?" Andrew insisted. He did have a point.

"I'll go," the nearly-inebriated Lord Asquith offered, quickly turning from the crumpled remains of Lady Algernon at the bottom of the stairwell.

Percy's lips thinned. "Very well."

Did Percy feel threatened by Andrew? He could have no real reason to—not anymore. Not since the Harrigans had lost their money and Andrew had broken our engagement. *Broken my heart.* No, Andrew had abandoned me. He didn't want me.

Though my feelings might have been a little more tender than I'd realized before coming face to face with Andrew Harrigan again.

But even so. There was no future with him. Percy could see this logic, couldn't he?

"I could use one of those scones," I said gently, squeezing lightly on Percy's bicep.

His demeanor softened. "Of course, darling." He led me away, but I couldn't help but glance back once.

Andrew's eyes were locked on me, pain, determination, and longing written on his face.

I ate an unladylike amount of scone and short pastry. It seemed that once food passed my lips, I morphed into a ravening beast. I wouldn't have eaten so much in front of Percy, but surely extenuating circumstances could account for my suddenly voracious appetite.

"Have another tumbler," Percy encouraged Lord Asquith. The man was so deep in his cups it was a miracle he was still able to get the drink to his lips. I couldn't fathom why Percy was encouraging him to imbibe more of the demon liquor.

A few short seconds later, Lord Asquith's head hit the table with a thud, a loud snore issuing from his lips. I daintily wiped my mouth with my napkin and took some water.

"Emma Grace, I wanted to speak to you privately," Percy whispered urgently.

My ears perked, instantly alert. "What is it?"

"I've been thinking, what if Lord Barclay left notes in his office—something about the poem that would give us insight—maybe even tell us who the murderer was?"

My lips parted in a silent O. "You mean, maybe tell who the killer is by his own hand—almost like a premonition?"

"Not necessarily a premonition, but he'd likely make notes or some such as he was preparing for the invites to go out from Mistlethwaite. If he arranged this all on his own, with only brief help from the Leonards—God rest their souls—then surely, he made commentary on his choices."

"Certainly," I said as hope and understanding dawned. "We must search his study." Could we discover who was behind these heinous murders?

"I don't trust anyone else," Percy said. "Let's go search now, while the others are engaged and cannot see us find the incriminating evidence."

A niggle of fear wiggled its way into my subconscious. What if I found something that further implicated Andrew? I shoved the thought away. I needed to know, once and for all, if my heart could be trusted.

Because my heart said he was innocent.

Percy beckoned me, and I rose quietly from the table, my skirts making far less noise without all the layers of petticoats. He grabbed my hand and tugged me through the corridor, skirting past the main entrance staircase that would have taken us past the blood stain left behind from the remains of Mr. Leonard's brain, and through the long, darkened hallways to the door of Lord Barclay's study.

I hesitated.

"Oh, I'm sorry, Emma Grace," Percy said, pinching the bridge of his nose. "I'm an insensitive clod. I didn't think about Lord Barclay still being in the room. Forgive my oversight. Do you wish to stay here at the door while I search?"

I swallowed. "No, I will be well. Besides, the searching will go twice as fast with two of us looking at the same time. Twice the ground," I babbled, not keen on seeing more dead bodies.

"You're sure?" Percy's thumb ran over the back of my knuckles.

I nodded. "I can do this."

"Very well. Let us hope we find something quickly."

Percy wrapped his fist around the doorknob and turned. But what met our eyes had me blinking in rapid succession, my heart picking up speed to match the frantic tempo.

There was no body upon the couch.

Lord Barclay's corpse was missing.

CHAPTER SEVENTEEN

I gasped, the noise loud enough it echoed in the stone hallway. "Where—" I swallowed. "Where is Lord Barclay?" My pulse hammered behind my eyeballs, practically making them jiggle in their sockets.

Percy took several long strides into the room, looking wildly about, just as shocked as I was. He searched under the couch, then the surrounding area.

Real fear lurked in Percy's eyes that sent a skitter of foreboding thumping up my spine.

"He—he *was* dead. I'm certain of it." Percy's face was white.

"Of course, he was dead. We all saw him; we all saw the knife protruding from his back. We all watched as his corpse was laid out on this very couch." I pointed to the dried bloodstain still evident on the camel-colored leather. There were a few drips below, dried on the carpet.

"We must find the others," Percy rasped.

I didn't disagree. I very much wanted Andrew and his gun in that moment.

We didn't tarry, all but running down the corridors back to the dining room. Lord Asquith was still snoring lightly with his head on the tabletop. Commotion sounded from the opposite corridor, and relief warred with the raw horror coating the back of my throat. The others were on their way to the dining room as well.

"Andrew," I said as his form appeared. I glanced at Percy, having forgotten to use Andrew's formal title in my shock. Thankfully, Percy didn't seem to notice my slip.

"What's wrong? Are you hurt?" Andrew took three bounding steps, grabbed my elbows, and looked me over.

I shook my head, half-heartedly attempting to pry his hands from my arms, though truthfully, I liked them there.

"Where is the gun?" Percy asked. His eyes were wild. Finding Lord Barclay missing must have shaken him more than he'd let on.

Andrew dropped his hold and stepped in front of me.

"I think you should surrender the gun," Mr. Campbell said. He, Mr. Angus, and Mrs. Wentworth were standing just inside the door near the sideboard.

"You're only miffed because I'd have had no compunction against using it on you," Andrew said. "I certainly won't be handing it over to you."

"Lord Fairfax, you look like you've seen a ghost," Mr. Angus said, then winced. "Sorry, bad timing on the use of the expression."

"But that's just it," I insisted. "Lord Barclay's body is missing."

All eyes focused on me.

"What?" Mr. Campbell said, eyes round as saucers.

"It's true. Percy and I were just at his study, and his body is gone."

Andrew's eyes narrowed at me as if to ask why we were at the study, alone, without the snoring Lord Asquith.

"What if he's not really dead?" Mrs. Wentworth whispered. "He's returned as a ghost. A vengeful spirit to take his wrath out on us!"

"What if he's the one that's been killing?" Mr. Angus said. "None of us saw Lady Algernon trip down the stairs. We just assumed. What if she was pushed? By Lord Barclay. In corporeal form, not as a spirit," he added with a glance at the white-faced Mrs. Wentworth.

"Could he have faked his own death to turn us all against each other?" Andrew suggested.

"But how...how could he? We all saw the wound. We—he was dead," Percy said.

"At least we all thought so," Mr. Campbell said, his entire demeanor uneasy.

Mr. Angus's brows drew together. Andrew's arm brushed mine and I took momentary delight in the heat it sent flashing to my extremities and the sense of protection his nearness evoked.

"There is one thing that yet perplexes me," Mr. Angus said.

"Only one?" Mr. Campbell snorted.

"The angle of the wound." He tapped his lip.

Andrew went rigid beside me, his head swinging to Mr. Angus. "He could not have made such a wound by himself."

William Angus nodded. "It would be nearly impossible. I noted how the blade was stuck into him, begging the ladies' pardon, but even if the man were ambidextrous, to shove a knife blade into one's own flesh to the hilt at such a strange angle, would be unmanageable."

"He had to have an accomplice," Andrew said, his voice low.

"Or there's someone else in the manor with us." Lord Asquith's words dropped like lead weights. The young lord raised his head, propping his chin in his hand, his elbow rudely on the table.

"Oh!" Mrs. Wentworth drew a shaking hand to her lips.

"Or one of us is in cahoots with him." Mr. Angus said.

Dread slithered in my gut.

"I still say it's one of you." Mr. Campbell crossed his arms, his eyes chips of flint as he pinned first me, then Percy, then Andrew.

"What prevents it from being you?" I retorted, emboldened with Andrew standing beside me.

"I had nothing to gain from killing him. Nor do I have anything to hide." He gave me a smarmy smile.

My cheeks heated and anger burbled beneath the surface as I knew how he'd interpret my flush—as a sign I *did* have something to hide.

"Enough," Mr. Angus said. "We need to go back to the scene. Let us examine where his body was and see if we can unearth any clues as to who is hunting us."

A chill gripped my shoulders. "Do you really think we're being hunted?" I whispered.

"I'm not sure what else you'd call this, " Mr. Angus's dark eyes held little fear, but great distrust.

I nodded. There was nothing else for us to do.

By unspoken agreement, one by one, we filed from the room. Andrew wrapped a hand around my arm.

"Wait, Emma Grace," he whispered. He pulled me back inside the dining room, out of sight of the others. My pulse picked up, though there was no proper reason it should.

"Here," he whispered again. Close enough his breath brushed the side of my face. He pressed something cold and hard into my hand. Glancing down, I nearly dropped it.

Andrew had put the gun in my hand and wrapped my fingers around it.

"Pull the hammer back, aim, and shoot. Preferably not me," he added with a wry grin. "If we're being hunted, and I think there is credence to Angus's words, I want you to be as protected as possible." His brown eyes were swimming in sincerity. "Tuck it into the waistband of your skirts. Your jacket will hide it well enough."

I nodded numbly.

"Now, Emma Grace," he said gently. "You need to hide it *now*. The others will wonder where we are."

That spurred me to action. Taking his advice, and heedless how he watched me closely, I pulled up my jacket, hesitated, then wedged the gun into my pocket instead.

"I can reach my pocket quicker than fumbling with my jacket."

He nodded in approval. I was thankful I'd put on the one petticoat with pockets. The bulk of my skirt would hide the weapon and all I needed to do was slip my hand through the slit in my skirts to reach it.

"Emma Grace? What are you doing? Back away from her," Percy demanded as his head appeared through the doorway of the dining room.

"I was merely ascertaining the lady's safety," Andrew said as he gallantly stepped back.

"*I* will keep her safe, thank you very much. Lady Hastings need not be any of your concern." Percy's voice bordered on condescending anger. "Come, Emma Grace."

Dutifully, I looped a hand through Percy's elbow and let him lead me from the room. Andrew followed at my back, his nearness sending newfangled electricity buzzing across my arms and raising gooseflesh from my shoulders to my ankles.

The gun thumped against my thigh.

CHAPTER
EIGHTEEN

The study remained bereft of Lord Barclay's corpse, though I wondered if perhaps his ghost *was* still in attendance, for a chill descended upon me as I entered the room. Once stately, it was filled with books and papers, a globe, gilded statuary, and a potted plant that was shivering near the window. But despite the warm trappings, it all felt cold and empty now. Literally and figuratively. I'd never before so wished to find a dead body.

We spread out in the room, the eight of us. Lady Fulbright sat on a wicker-backed chair, her eyes staring listlessly at the floor. I hadn't heard her speak since Lady Algernon expired at the end of the stairwell. I didn't blame her. How horrible to think your lover the murderer only to be in fear for your mortal life, then watch said lover expire against the corner of a dressing table. I thought perhaps she'd suffered through more than the rest of us since we'd been at Mistlethwaite Manor, though at least she was still living. More than could be said of her erstwhile lover.

Mrs. Wentworth set upon a wooden file holder with a vengeance. I assumed she sought information on the wool trade, and Lord Barclay's involvement in it. It was obvious she blamed our absent host for her husband's suicide.

Percy had torn apart the couch where we'd put Lord Barclay's body. The leather cushions he cast on the floor; he even crawled beneath it to look at the underside.

"Ah ha!" Mr. Campbell crowed as he stood at the bookshelves. He tugged one tome back and a section of wall pulled away to reveal a massive safe set into the wall.

"By George," Lord Asquith said, eyes growing wide with greed. He practically salivated as he took in the metal door of the safe.

"I guess we know where the ten thousand pounds is being kept," Andrew quipped. He hadn't strayed far from my side but gave the illusion of space to pacify Percy. While I appreciated his gesture, I was still caught in a tug of war between the two. My old love and my new almost-betrothed. Even if that was ridiculous. Or so my brain told me. My heart was having a different conversation.

"Not that anyone can get into the safe to retrieve it. I doubt if figuring out the puzzle would produce the prize at this point," Mr. Angus mused.

We continued searching the room for any new clues for several minutes.

"This is hopeless. Anything he might have had here has either been moved, or it was never here in the first place," Mr. Angus said with a huff. "And it's painfully obvious his body is no longer here, and we have found no scrap of information as to its current whereabouts."

"Hideous man," Mrs. Wentworth mumbled.

"He did say he had eyes all over his manor," Mr. Campbell said disdainfully. "Maybe some of them spirited him away."

The shadows outside lengthened, and to my delight, I realized the storm was starting to abate. "Look," I said, crossing to one of the large windows. Snow flurries still raced, but at half the speed as before. I could see through the gusting flakes beyond the window into a world of white, lit up in fiery reds and pinks as the sun set.

"We should be able to leave tomorrow," Andrew said softly from over my shoulder. I shivered at his nearness.

"How I wish it could be tonight," I confessed.

"I agree, but we'd only freeze to death out of doors. It's a more certain way to die than staying in these cursed walls one more night."

I shivered again, this time thinking about the rose. "What if someone breaks into my room again," I whispered.

"I'll come. I'll stand watch."

"That would be most improper," I chided, mostly because it was the polite response.

"Do you think I'd besmirch your character or do anything untoward?" he asked, his breath brushing tendrils across my neck.

"No."

"Would you prefer your pomaded peacock?"

"Don't call him that," I said on a sigh.

"You didn't answer my question," he insisted.

I was supposed to say yes. I was supposed to desire Percy's company above all others. He was meant to be my refuge, my protector, my dearest love.

Then why did the thought of Percy in my rooms all night do nothing but invoke irritation?

I tried to call up the old anger toward Andrew. To bring his betrayal to mind. Surely that would give me some perspective.

It didn't. All it produced was a sadness for what I'd once had and lost.

What if my heart was trapped in the past...with Andrew? What then of my future?

Footsteps sounded—Percy's, by the gait. "Why must you insist in your unwanted attentions? I told you Lady Hastings is none of your concern." He bit out the words.

"I did not know it was a crime to look out a window. Particularly as one might ascertain the ability to leave or not. Look. The snow is slowing."

I could hear the steel undertones in Andrew's voice. *Looking at the snow, my right eye.* He'd been looking at me, and I knew it. The errant thought tugged the corner of my mouth up.

"We should rejoin the others," I said, schooling my features and doing my best to head off the impending argument between the two men. I walked toward the door of the study, not waiting for them to follow, but assuming that they would. Hoping they would. Regardless of my tangled emotions, I felt safer with one or both of them near than I did without. Even with the gun heavy in my pocket.

My footfalls were muffled by the carpet runner of the hallway. Nearing the door of the library, I paused, something flickering at the back of my mind as I caught sight of a portrait. The waning daylight from the window set high in the corridor illuminated just enough that I could make out fine features, silky brown hair, and familiar eyes.

Stepping inside the room, I noted the library had an updated light fixture. Rummaging a bit, I located matches and a taper in a drawer under the gas lamp. Lighting the taper, I held it up to the fixture. The gas mantle ignited with a *pop*. I waited for it to burn hot enough to shed light into the darkening room while the rest of the guests crowded in behind me.

"What are you doing in here?" Mrs. Wentworth asked, her haughty condescension back in full display.

I crossed the room slowly, cocking my head to the side as I gazed at the portrait. It must have been commissioned a few decades in the past because the style was Impressionism, which had found its height shortly before I was born. The painting was of a girl, younger than me. Even with the quick, hard brush strokes of the painter, there was something eerily familiar about the woman.

"Is that Lady Algernon?" Percy asked.

The familiarity clicked. The eyes, the hair, the shape of the face. Though the painting was in a less than realistic style, and the woman I had known so briefly was much aged, the resemblance was remarkable.

And that wasn't all.

My eyes whipped to Mr. Campbell, who also bore a striking resemblance to the woman in the painting. Not as much to the older Lady Algernon, but enough that I still probably should have seen it when she was living. But seeing the painting, Mr. Campbell, and having seen the older Lady Algernon, the resemblance was undeniable.

"You're the spitting image," Mr. Angus said, his gaze going from the design and back to Mr. Campbell.

"No," Mr. Campbell said unevenly. "I—I'm from North Umbria. My parents are Frank and Minnie Campbell." He tugged on the collar of his shirt.

"I wouldn't be too sure about that," Andrew mumbled.

"You! What are you doing?" Mrs. Wentworth shrieked.

As one, we turned, only to find Lord Asquith with several items of differing value, some half-stuffed into his pockets, some nearly there. He sputtered, though no actual words came out.

"You little thief," Mr. Campbell said.

Lord Asquith straightened his spine. "It's not as if anyone can possibly win the prize money now. Barclay is missing, and it's not as if he's going to miss it. Look at this place!"

"That doesn't give you license to help yourself," Percy insisted.

Mrs. Wentworth huffed. "Besides, we no longer have Lord Barclay's body. He may very well be alive. Remember when he said he had eyes all over Mistlethwaite Manor? What if he's watching us right this moment. You may be next to perish! You conniving little robber!" She drew herself to her full height and pointed a long finger at him.

Lord Asquith paled. "I—surely he's not."

"But what if he is?" I whispered mostly to myself.

Mrs. Wentworth continued. "And you," she said to Mr. Campbell, "don't think we're done with you. Who is Rose Algernon to you? You can be nothing beyond her flesh and blood. Look at the resemblance!"

"What if this is all more fodder to get us to figure out the poem? What if he really does want us to determine who fits who in the poem? Perhaps he means to reappear once we've solved it," Mr. Angus said.

His words jerked the poem back to the forefront of my mind. Without any desire to do so, the ditty flooded my brain.

Two are staff, here to serve,
Our merriment to preserve.

One of you has been bamboozled
One of you is worthless, utterly foozled

One born on the wrong side of the sheets
Two of you, your spouses properly fleeced

For one of you, business has been bad
One of you, your innocence's been had

One of you is a commoner—just polite
One of you a child, innocent not quite

One has been wronged, taken a long fall
Only one is the Master of it all."

The first two lines had to pertain to the Leonards. Though they weren't preserving any merriment at the moment. I still wasn't sure who had been bamboozled or foozled. But I now had sneaking suspicions that perhaps it was Mr. Campbell who had been born on the wrong side of the sheets. And given his remarkable resemblance to the young Rose Algernon—who had admitted to me that she and Horace Barclay had likely once been involved, could she be the one whose innocence had been had? By Horace Barclay? Could Mr. Campbell be the offspring of Rose Algernon and Horace Barclay in their youth? Was that why she had to flee to the Continent and marry so quickly once she returned?

Scandal tingled in the tips of my fingers. Oh, what a tangled web of deceit. But still. Considering that it wasn't *my* innocence being discussed was a welcome recollection. Assuming I was correct in my deductions. "Mr. Campbell, what year were you born?" I asked, oblivious to the arguments carrying on around me.

"As if I should tell you anything about me, you little vixen," he shot back at me.

Percy lunged for Mr. Campbell, and shock rooted me to the spot where I stood beneath the portrait. Percy's fist connected with Mr. Campbell's jaw, the crack of it resounding in the stillness of the room. Mr. Campbell reared back two steps, bloody spittle flying from his lip. "You bracket-faced fumbler!" Mr. Campbell shouted as his hand flew to his jaw. A collective gasp rose from a few of us at his crass language, nearly as shocking as the fight breaking out in front of us. He charged Percy, knocking into him and crashing the both of them into the unforgiving side of a wingbacked chair. They shoved close to Lord Asquith and the younger man was too slow to get out of the way, taking a backhanded punch across the face as Mr. Campbell yanked his arm back to deliver another strike.

"Why you—" The young lord didn't finish his insult, merely jumped into the fray, the three men thrashing around.

"Andrew, do something," I pleaded.

"I'm not sure who to help, who to save, or who to thump," he said, his face showing his confusion as the three men wrestled.

"You get Lord Fairfax. I'll go after Campbell. Asquith will work himself out. He's still half squiffed," Mr. Angus said.

"Right. Here we go." Andrew took off his jacket and handed it to me, readying to jump into the fray. A wet, meaty sound splashed through the air. Grunts and a few moans sounded as Mr. Angus and Andrew ran to diffuse the angry brawl, but just as they reached the fight there was a hissing flicker, a *pop*, and then the room was shrouded in total blackness as the gas mantle fizzled out and crumbled.

A gunshot tore through the room, the blaze from the barrel momentarily blinding me. A groan rippled gooseflesh up my arms as my hands clapped over my mouth. A scream worked its way up my throat and added to the cacophony of noise and chaos surrounding me.

Andrew!

Andrew!

Andrew!

A gust of frigid wind barreled into the room, any noises associated with it drowned out by the keening of women and shouts of men. A window sash crashed back into its setting and the gusting freeze ceased.

"The taper! Someone light the taper!"

The taper. Yes! Light, we needed light! The gas mantle in the fixture was obviously done for, but the taper would at least give us small illumination. And that was better than none. I fumbled my way back toward where I thought the door was, the barest smudge of gray light filtering in through the library doorway. My hip found the edge of the table where the matches and taper had been, and I winced at the dull ache it caused. Ignoring the pain, I wedged my hand into the drawer and retrieved the waxy taper and tin of matches.

Flame whisked to light as the tiny match caught the wick of the candle. I held it high, illuminating as big a circle as the one tiny candle could muster.

"Who is hurt?" I called out, my voice still lost in the sea of other noises.

My eyes found Andrew in the dark and I breathed a sigh of relief that he was still standing.

"I'm shot!" Mr. Campbell hollered, staggering away from the group of bloodied men. He gripped his shoulder, and I could make out a trickle of blood welling through his fingers.

Mr. Angus appeared next in the cacophony of faces. He hauled Lord Asquith to his feet.

"Percy!" I cried. He was huddled near the fireplace, a smudge on the ground. I took a step toward him before the angry venom in Mr. Campbell's voice stopped me.

"You shot me!" Mr. Campbell shouted, pointing his good arm at Andrew.

Andrew slowly raised his hands as a new sort of fear slithered down my spine. Andrew didn't have the gun. I did. And I hadn't fired it.

There was another deadly weapon in our presence.

CHAPTER NINETEEN

P ercy raised his head, moaning.

Andrew, keeping Mr. Campbell's pointing finger and accusations within his gaze, reached down to lend an arm to Percy to help.

"Are you injured?" Andrew asked Percy.

"Get away from me! Where's the gun? Someone get the scoundrel, Harrigan!" Percy called, shoving himself to his feet and unsteadily backing a few steps toward the window, putting distance between himself and Andrew.

"Mr. Harrigan, I think it'd be best if you turned over the gun now," Mr. Angus said in a soothing voice.

Andrew smiled bitterly, wiping a drip of blood from near his eyebrow. "I don't have it."

"Of course you have it. We all saw you threaten me with it earlier!" Mr. Campbell cried, saliva flying from the corners of his mouth. "And now you've bloody *shot* me!"

Andrew shook his head slowly, catching my eye and continuing to shake his head. He wanted me to stay quiet. I bit the inside of my cheek. Hard.

"I *did* have it, yes. But I hid it. It is no longer in my possession."

"You liar," Percy seethed.

Andrew turned steely eyes on my intended. "Search me, then, if you don't believe me." Andrew held his arms up for everyone's inspection.

"Mr. Angus, if you'd do the honors?" Andrew asked.

"I'll do it," Percy said, a little too much glee mixed with the anger in his tone.

"I think your temper is a bit short. Angus has a cooler head. I'd rather he do it," Andrew insisted.

"I think the two of you are planning things together," Mr. Campbell said through clenched teeth. "The two of you! Maybe one of you is in league with Barclay. The other will end up as a patsy. But the two of you. I swear you're in on this together." What two? Percy and Andrew? The thought of the two of them in cahoots was laughable.

"Stop it. I'll search him." The words dropped from my mouth without my permission. I regretted them the moment they were out.

Percy turned pained eyes to me.

"Oh, that's rich, coming from you, it is," Lord Asquith said.

"Nothing you haven't seen before, hmmm?" Mrs. Wentworth added her venom.

"Shut up," Percy growled.

"Have Lady Fulbright do it," Lord Asquith said.

"She's already killed one man. I'd prefer she not," Andrew said, jaw ticking.

My heart raced, eyes watering.

"Have him undress in front of everyone then," Mr. Angus said.

"The impropriety!" Mrs. Wentworth shrieked.

"Woman, in case you haven't noticed, we're well past the bounds of propriety," Mr. Campbell said.

"Fine." Andrew started on the buttons of his shirt, his gaze flitting to me.

Red stained my cheeks, and the taper shook in my hand.

I couldn't watch this.

I couldn't look away.

"For mercy's sake, turn around, you wonton girl!" Mrs. Wentworth railed at me—notably with Andrew's body still in her peripheral vision.

"You will *not* speak to Lady Hastings in such a way," Percy thundered.

"And why not? I still say she's the one what's lost her ! Pure, virginal appearances can be deceiving. I've seen how she looks at you and him behind your backs. She's playing you both and giving out all her favors to stay ahead." She smiled wickedly, the weak light bouncing off her teeth.

Blood rushed from my head and black dots danced heavily in front of my eyes.

"She is not," Andrew said with deadly calm. His fists clenched tight enough one knuckle popped audibly. His shirt was fully unbuttoned, leaving his torso exposed. Faint shadows outlined the ridges of his stomach.

"How dare you!" Percy started, fists clenched and pumping the air once before whirling and exploding on Andrew. "Well, *did* you steal her innocence?"

I thought I might faint. This was all too much. Did Percy truly question my virginity? Clearly, Percy had been stewing in these thoughts for some time to have such an eruption. My innocence...was nearly completely intact. Guilt and outrage clawed at my throat, cutting off my air, and keeping all my words trapped inside me. Could this nightmare get any worse? Thoughts spun inside my brain, whirling without mercy.

Was this somehow my fault? The taper wavered harder, wax dotting the floor.

"Of course, *she's innocent*. Do you think her father would have let me live if the situation had been otherwise?" Andrew's voice rose in volume as anger glinted in his eyes.

"But are *you* innocent?" Percy roared back. "What did you take that should have been mine? While we're on the subject, what else have you taken in the past twenty-four hours? *Have you taken life*?"

Tears obscured my vision, and a vice closed around my airway. I blew out the candle, dropped it and Andrew's jacket, and fled the room, alone, into the darkness.

Which was possibly the most foolish thing I'd ever done.

When my breaths came in tight gasps and reason returned, I stood utterly forsaken in a darkened gallery filled with statuary. Some contorted as if in rage, some in shame, some in anger. Perhaps my own feelings were clouding my vision, but I saw no joy or happiness among the stone faces. Bright moonlight shivered through the snow still swirling lazily outside two large windows and illuminated the planes of hopelessness carved into each expression.

I knew how the forgotten statuary felt.

I had no idea how those of us remaining would survive the night.

It was entirely possible that tonight was my last night on this earth. And as I had no desire to remain at the mercy of whoever might find me, I curled up into an alcove shrouded behind heavy drapery and hidden from view. I stared into the whirling white through the window and let my mind rehash things.

My heart ached as Percy's words—his questioning of my innocence—burned into my memory. He had every right to question me as I had very much given away my first kiss to Andrew Harrigan. A kiss Percival Crofton would have expected me to save for him.

Anger bumped into the ache. If Percy thought so little of me, how could he still seek my hand? Or was he done pursuing me?

I sniffed, muffling the noise with my sleeve. My mother would have apoplexy if she knew I'd just wiped snot onto the expensive velveteen.

Oh, Percy. My future with him had looked so bright. As I thought about Lord Fairfax and what his proposal would mean for me, there was no spark of joy. No bubbles desperately trying to escape the confines of my corset. He was assurance. He was the proper thing. He was sociably acceptable, and what was expected. He was exactly the sort of man I *should* marry.

I drew a shuddering breath. But he was not the man I wanted.

Caramel-colored hair and brown eyes crinkled at the edges swam before my mind's eye. Memories soaked in laughter, light, and joy wrapped around my heart like a warm embrace. Days spent in the sun, fingers fluttering, secret touches light as air against my wrist, my elbow. One kiss that had forever changed my life.

Andrew Harrigan.

He had been imprinted on my soul in a way that I could never change. Even if I were to fall in love a thousand times over, Andrew Harrigan would always be my first love. The one that still beat inside my heart in hidden places. The one I still craved.

I shook my head as silent tears welled and dribbled down my cheeks. How could I have ever thought Andrew the murderer? It was as if scales had fallen from my eyes, letting me see things clearly.

I believed Andrew. Believed that he would not murder. Believed that he desired to keep me safe. Desperately hoped that he might still desire me, despite my abominable treatment of him.

I exhaled a shaky breath, steeling my resolve. It was time I took my fate into my own hands.

I was done with Percival Crofton. Even if Andrew wanted nothing more to do with me, my heart still belonged to him. I wouldn't give it away to another so lightly. I'd been told all my life that I was a mere woman, that I should let my father, brothers, and someday, my husband make my decisions for me.

But no more.

As of this very second, I determined to set my own course. No one could have foreseen the horrendous turn of events the weekend had taken. As much as it had been ingrained to rely on the men around me, it was time to shirk those thoughts and become the mistress of my fate.

I started to rise, but every extremity froze as footfalls sounded at the far end of the rows of statuary. Biting the inside of my cheek, I sank back and silently curled my skirts around me, making myself as tiny and as obscure as possible, completely sheltered behind the draperies. My finger curved around the butt of the gun still in my pocket.

"Emma Grace. It's Andrew. I'm alone." The whispered words carried, rustling around carved muscle and shadowed figures like ghosts.

My heart seized in my chest. "Andrew," I whispered back. I forced air into my lungs as my fingers unclenched.

"Where are you?" His paces quickened, his voice still soft.

Struggling to my feet, I tripped on the hem of my skirt and pitched forward, wildly trying to catch my balance.

"I've got you." Andrew grunted as he caught the brunt of my fall against his chest.

We stood there, locked together with his hands around my waist and my arms smashed against his chest. He searched my face, his wreathed in concern.

"You've been crying."

I nodded.

"I'm so sorry, Emma Grace. Sorry for it all. Before we all split up to look for you, I let Percival know he's being an utter fool. That there is nothing between us. I'm sorry those nasty things were said about you. None of them are true." He sighed heavily, his breath brushing the escaped tendrils curling about my face. "I assured Percy of your innocence. That he has no fear on that account." The scant light showed a pained expression cross his face, and certainty settled in my bones.

If I was to die tonight, I wanted to die with Andrew knowing that I still loved him, and that I did not think him the murderer. Andrew Harrigan was an honorable man. Capable of killing? Yes. I thought so of my own self as well. But not murder. Not this cold-blooded escapade that was happening all around us. I trusted Andrew. And now I knew my feelings for him could not be ignored.

I reached up, grasping Andrew's face with both my hands, and drew it down to mine, my lips capturing his in a breathtaking kiss.

Determination bloomed afresh in my chest. I could not marry Percy Crofton. I *would not* marry Percy Crofton. Not while my heart beat for another. Andrew's abject poverty be cursed.

Andrew froze for a moment beneath the pressure of my lips, but then his hands wound farther round my waist, snugging me to him. His mouth came alive, and suddenly, I was not the aggressor of the kiss. His lips were warm and gentle, though assertive.

A sigh somersaulted up my throat but was swallowed as Andrew bent his head, his lips moving over mine. His hands tightened on the small of my back, drawing me even closer as one of my hands tangled into the hair at the base of his head while the other cupped his strong jaw, covered lightly in scruff. The rough feel of the tiny hairs beneath my fingers set my insides quivering, as did his hand that moved to the bottom of my ribs.

A low noise sounded at the back of his throat and my knees quite literally went weak. I didn't waste time worrying over my feeble joints, because Andrew held me up, pressed against his chest, kissing me with equal reverence and ardor.

He gasped, breaking his lips away, but leaning his forehead against mine. "Emma Grace." His voice was gravelly and full of desire.

"Andrew," I gasped back, thoroughly winded.

"Why on earth would you kiss me now?"

"Because if this is to be my last night, I wanted it to be spent in the knowledge that I told you once and for all that my heart belongs to you. I gave it to you years ago, and I never got it back." I hiccoughed as tears beaded on my lower lashes.

"This will not be your last night. I forbid it." His tone brooked no argument. But then he softened, the pad of his thumb tracing my jaw as he leaned back only far enough so I could see his eyes in the light from the moon shining through the window that reached our hidden corner of the world.

"I have never stopped loving you," he confessed, turning my insides to jelly.

"Then why did you leave me? Did you think I'd not want you without your family's money?"

His face shuttered and his shoulders rose and fell on a deep sigh.

"Andrew, please," I whispered. I cupped his jaw, raising his gaze to mine.

His brown eyes fixed on me, anguished, and searching. "Emma Grace, your father refused to let me see you." He swallowed hard and took a step back. "And he was right to do so. Never mind my feelings for you, I could not provide for you in the manner you should be kept."

My mouth gaped open in a most unlady-like fashion. "Father refused..."

Andrew nodded miserably. "With the loss of my family's money, there was no advantage at all to your father or for you to be tied to me. You deserve a man who can care for you properly. Not one who has been selling off family jewels and paintings to keep his family fed and in their ancestral home."

"Andrew." My heart cracked at his admission. "Did you not once think about what *I* wanted? What if *I* still wanted *you*?"

He did not answer, but instead slid his hand from my jaw to cradle the back of my head, much as he had the day so long ago in the hedge maze. He covered my lips again in a kiss that reached my very soul. My mouth opened, and for one shocked instant, our tongues collided. We hung there in a moment suspended before slowly, deliberately, mutually deepening the kiss. Tentatively exploring this exciting foreign territory. For long glorious minutes, the horrors of the evening fell away—the world fell away. There was nothing beyond the two of us, the breaths we shared, the love blooming afresh between us, and the passion rising like a powerful tide.

At last, we pulled apart. I wasn't sure if I was still on the ground or if I floated somewhere in bright clouds.

"I've missed you so much." Andrew groaned.

"So much," I echoed.

"I swear, Emma Grace, when this nightmare is over, I will do everything in my power to be worthy of you, to deserve you, and to make your father proud of me—enough that he will grant me his daughter's hand in marriage."

"If he doesn't, then we will elope to Gretna Green."

Andrew's head came up, eyes twinkling, and a smile tugging at his most kissable lips. "That would be a scandal of the highest magnitude."

I let my palms slide down the roughness of his jaws once more, delighting at the texture and angles of his face. "Andrew Harrigan. We've already been engaged once and broken things off. I've since been courted by Percy Crofton. Your family has lost your fortune, and if word of this night ever gets out, an elopement to Gretna Green will pale in comparison."

His smile fell slightly. "Would you truly leave it all—to be with me?"

"I would." And I meant it.

"Truly?" he asked again, hope lighting his eyes.

"Truly. I want nothing more than to be your wife. To love you, to hold you, to be loved and held in return." Tears pricked the back of my eyes again.

"Oh, Emma Grace," he murmured. He drew me close, one hand tight around my back, the other firm against my waist. He held me, loving me. I drew a breath, relishing his minty scent, my heart at last content with its other half.

I pulled back first. Only because I wanted to kiss him once more. I couldn't seem to stop myself. Pandora's Box had been unlatched, and all my dreams and wishes were floating away from the tight confines in which they'd been kept. Everything I desired orbited Andrew Harrigan.

I could feel his longing through his lips and my own desire rushed to meet it, but Andrew broke the kiss, a smirk tipping his mouth.

"I guess you've made a liar of me," he said with a low chuckle.

"You've never been a liar, Andrew Harrigan."

"Yes, but I just told Lord Percival Crofton there was nothing between us. Clearly, there is."

I snorted. "Well, at the time there was only heartbreak and hope. Now there is something tangible."

He smiled down at me and nodded. "Then if your father still withholds his blessing, and you're sure you still want me after this mess, we will go to Gretna Green."

"I will always want you."

He kissed me lightly once more. "Then let's find a way to solve this wretched puzzle, end these murders, and quit this place."

"Agreed."

CHAPTER TWENTY

"I keep thinking," Andrew started, his fingers twining with mine as we whispered in the alcove, still hidden from the rest of the manor, and I hoped from any of Lord Barclay's spying eyes. "I agree with Lord Fairfax, much as I'm loathe to admit it. There should be a paper trail somewhere. Unless he burned all his evidence, and I find that unlikely as he'd need proof in order to blackmail all the guests, so it must be here somewhere. It's possible it's in the safe, in which case we're just out of luck until the police can come take charge. With the weather as it is, we should be able to leave to get help tomorrow, though we're still several miles from the nearest anything."

"We searched his study today though. No body and no papers."

Andrew rubbed his thumbs across the back of my knuckles, and I feared my knees might collapse beneath me.

"I found a single drop of blood."

"How does that help us? There was a dried puddle of it by the couch."

Andrew smirked. "Yes. But I found a drop on the floor of the interior wall. On the opposite side of the wall that hid the safe."

It took me a moment to catch up with his train of thought, but when I did, it hit me like a stick between the eyes. "Andrew, you're brilliant."

"I have moments. Like this one." Without further warning, but slow enough I could pull back if I wanted to, he dipped his head, and caught my lips once more in a sweet, lingering kiss.

"If you keep doing that, we'll never get any sleuthing done." Was I certain I still wanted to sleuth if kissing Andrew was the alternative?

"A fair point. We'll make up for lost time soon enough." He placed a last gentle kiss on my forehead.

"So, back to the study then?"

"Provided we can keep clear of the other guests to get there. At least one of us *is* a murderer. It wasn't me, and it wasn't you. I'm not keen to rejoin their society."

"You trust no one?"

"I trust you. But my list ends there."

"You trusted me to go with Percy earlier," I countered.

"Correction. I trusted that he would not harm *you*. I'm not certain of his innocence." His expression turned sour. "I hated seeing you go with him."

"Is that a note of jealousy I detect, Mr. Harrigan?" I teased.

"More than a note, Lady Hastings. Try: 'twas entirely insufferable to watch you with him," he confessed.

A deliciously poignant ache bloomed inside my chest. "I never kissed Percy Crofton," I whispered.

Andrew's grin spread across his whole face. "That *is* a good piece of news. And I'm very glad to hear it. It might have driven me mad, wondering if I compared well to his lordship."

"I hardly think you need a boost to your ego." I smiled through my words.

"Still. It's the sort of thing a man would think about."

"A woman would, too," I said around the ball of emotion rising in the back of my throat.

"I've never kissed anyone save you either, Emma Grace."

I grinned like a fool.

"Unless you count the cheeks of mothers, aunts, or sisters."

I swatted his arm.

"Emma Grace," his body stilled, and my nerves were instantly on high alert.

"What?"

"Do you see a pin prick of light over there?"

He gently turned my face so that I was pointed in the correct direction. He was right. There was the barest prick of light coming from a patch of wainscoting.

"The wainscoting. Could it be another hidden servant's entrance? But why would he need one here? In a dusty, old, forgotten statuary menagerie?"

"He wouldn't," Andrew said with certainty.

"I think we should take a closer look." Boldness laced my words. I was nearly giddy with these new emotional revelations and the decision to have a heavier hand in my own future.

"Agreed. You still have the gun?"

"I do." I patted my pocket where the weapon lay concealed.

"Do you trust me?"

"With all of my heart."

"Good. Let's go do some investigating."

CHAPTER
TWENTY-ONE

Our hunch proved correct. After finding a button in a knot of wood in the paneling—something we'd probably never have found had we not been looking with our fingers in the darkness—a secret door opened to us, revealing a lone old-fashioned gas light. The light was only just hanging on, flickering, a line of soot-stain blackening the wall and ceiling. With no gas mantle that would easily break and crumble, thus ensuring it would be around when someone most needed to sneak through hidden passageways, it was rather clever. We stepped inside the cramped passage, and Andrew quickly shut the secret panel behind us, lest anyone else happen upon our discovery and follow us into the unknown.

Thrill and foreboding warred for prominence as my toes wiggled in agitation.

Wordlessly, I passed Andrew the gun from my pocket and nodded that he should go first. He winked and took up a protective stance, shielding me with his body as he went ahead of me down the passage.

The dim passage seemed to stretch half of forever. Every so often we'd come to doors, all of them complete with peepholes. Horace Barclay really *could* have had spies all over the manor. If he himself, or trusted servants, had used these passages, they could have accumulated all manner of incriminating information. Doubtless, they did. Maybe Lord Barclay still *was* gathering intelligence. That was a disturbing thought. I didn't relish the idea of running into the horrible man in the darkness of a hidden passageway. I was more grateful than ever that Andrew had happened upon Mrs. Wentworth's gun.

It was by these peepholes that we were able to orient ourselves within the manor. When we came to stairs, we realized we had quick access to our bedrooms. It was also the ready explanation for how the rose had come to lay on my nightstand. The question of who exactly had put it there remained a mystery.

"Where should we search next?" Andrew whispered as we came back down to the base of the simple staircase that led to the guest chambers.

"Let's go back to the study." I wanted to see where that drop of blood Andrew found could lead us. Though I was loathe to find Lord Barclay. I suspected he was hiding away, masterminding this whole macabre plot.

"Agreed." His fingers brushed from my elbow to my fingertips, sending a jolt of electric current flashing through my extremities.

It took some meandering through the winding hidden hallways, but eventually, we found the library, and the study should have been merely one more door down.

Andrew's hand suddenly flew out behind him, halting me in my tracks. My heart drummed as we held perfectly still.

A ripping sound made its way faintly to our ears. Silently, Andrew shifted, giving me access to the peephole. The library was shrouded in shadow, more dark than light, and we weren't positioned well in the wall to see the person or persons present in the room. The ripping sound continued, and muttered words accompanied it.

"You are *not* my mother. I won't allow it. You will not be my shame anymore."

It had to be Mr. Campbell. But where was everyone else?

Andrew tapped my hand and jerked his head that we should continue. My low heel clicked softly against the plank flooring.

"Who's there? Show yourself!" Mr. Campbell said, panic lacing his tone.

Wincing and silently cursing my low-heeled shoes, I leaned down and quickly removed them. On noiseless footfalls, we left the vicinity of the library and edged toward the study.

We rounded a corner where another barely lit gas lamp cast illu-mination around us, and Andrew stopped so suddenly I collided into his back. His muscles were taut, rigid beneath his jacket. I wasn't even sure if he was breathing.

I rolled to the balls of my feet and glanced over his shoulder, then immediately wished I hadn't.

There, face down on the floor, lay Lord Barclay. He clutched the bloody knife in his hand. He must have pulled it from his back himself. So much blood had pooled and dried into a wicked stain beneath him, black and shiny in the scant light of the gas light hanging above the entrance to...wait. The study should be on the opposite wall of this door.

"I guess he really is dead," Andrew said after several heartbeats. "He must have only lost consciousness in the initial attack. I assume he came to sometime later, tried to make it to this secret place, removed the knife, then passed out from blood loss, and died here on the floor."

I nodded against his shoulder. My eyes darted to the door—there was one right there where a hidden entrance to the study should be. But here, where Lord Barclay's arm was out-stretched, there was another door.

A hidden door within a hidden passage.

"Brace yourself. I'm opening the door," Andrew whispered, reaching for the unexpected door. He gripped the gun, aiming it at whatever might be on the other side.

I held my breath.

CHAPTER
TWENTY-TWO

A ndrew edged the door open on well-oiled hinges. The gas light from the hallway gave enough illumination to quickly ascertain that the tiny room was empty. A desk, a set of drawers, an inkwell, a jumble of papers on the desk, and an oil lamp crowded into my focus. A chair sat askew behind the desk, as if its occupant had gotten up and left in a hurry. I glanced back at Lord Barclay's corpse. Had he been trying to reach this secret room to hide? Conceal himself from his attacker?

It appeared he never made his escape. He might have been a reprehensible man, but it was utterly cruel to see death in this way. This reaching for life, for safety, only to crash and expire on the floor, an arm's length short of the goal. Although, even if he had reached the safety of his secret lair, I doubted it could have offered him any life sustaining measures. I gulped as I involuntarily glanced back at his too-still form in the hallway. The faint bluish pallor of his skin, purpling near where he laid against the floor. There was no denying he was good and truly dead this time. I turned away.

"I think we're alone. Let's light the lamp and shut the door, just in case," Andrew whispered. I nodded and quickly entered the little room. There was scarcely space for the two of us to turn around together in the tight confines.

Quickly, I located a match tin and struck a light, carefully taking off the glass globe of the oil lamp and lighting the wick. Once the globe was back in place, I turned the wick up enough for the single lamp to cast light over the whole room.

"I'll start at the cabinet, and you take the desk?" Andrew asked, tucking the gun into the waistband of his pants.

"Here's to hoping we find something," I said as I made my way around the littered desk and seated myself in the chair. Before I started riffling through Lord Barclay's papers, I glided my heeled slippers back onto my frigid stocking-clad feet.

Raising my head from securing my shoes, my breath caught as the soft lamp light cast a warm glow on a single photograph on the edge of the desk.

Carefully, I picked it up. It was a very young Lady Algernon and a tiny babe. My thumb ran gently over the curve of the infant's face. Curious, I worked the back of the frame off to see the back of the picture. There, in elegant script on the back was a short inscription.

Rose Howard and Clarance

In Horace Barclay's script was written two words below: *Our son*

"Andrew, I think this might be Clarance Campbell—Rose Algernon's son...and Horace Barclay's."

Andrew glanced over and I angled the picture so he could see it. His eyebrows rose and a soft *whoosh* of air passed his lips. "Guess that solves another mystery. We thought Campbell was Lady Algernon's son, but I'd say this confirms that Barclay was his father for certain. What a mess that one man made."

I nodded, full in agreement. Andrew turned back to the drawers, and I gently put the photograph back and turned my attention to the desk.

Gazing down, all I could make out was a mish mash of chicken scratch, doodles, ink blots, and random bits of poetry. But the poetry struck a chord. Perhaps he'd worked on his dreadful poem here at this very desk. There'd been no evidence in the library when we'd searched, so maybe he kept his unscrupulous dealings away from public eyes and handled matters here. I started sorting and organizing. Clearly, the man would have benefited from a secret secretary for his horrendous business. Useless information went into one pile, correspondence into another, and then, under the tenth or twelfth paper, I found something useful.

It was a piece of common paper, but at the top of it was printed *LORD RAYMOND VILLIERS*, and under it was a short list:

Having affair with Lady Francis Fulbright.

Lord Fulbright does not care, provided discretion is used.

Lady V does mind. American heiress. Brought one million pounds to the marriage. Tied up in a prenuptial agreement. She keeps the money if V. is unfaithful and it can be proved in a court of law. Legal and binding.

LORD RAYMOND VILLERS

Having affair with Lady Francis Fulbright.

Lord Fulbright does not care provided discretion is used

Lady V does mind.
   American heiress.
   Brought one million pounds to the marriage.
   Tied up in a prenuptial agreement.
   She keeps the money if V. is unfaithful and it
      can be proved in a court of law.
   Legal and binding.

"Oh, my gracious," I murmured.

"Did you find something?" Andrew turned from the file he was flipping through.

I passed him the document. Andrew's eyebrows hiked to his hairline.

"Angus hit that square on the nose. Wonder how he knows about such things. Didn't he say he was common as common gets?"

"He did," I mused, "but perhaps there is more to him than meets the eye. He was invited here, after all, and it doesn't appear that Lord Barclay did many things out of the goodness of his heart."

"No, it would not," Andrew agreed.

We continued searching.

"Huh," Andrew said at length.

"What is it?"

"It appears your would-be fiancé is far more romantic than I would have credited him."

"Percy? What do you have?" A twinge of something akin to guilt pinged in my chest.

"It's a letter addressed to The Master of Mistlethwaite. Percy is asking him if he'd be willing to invite you for the weekend so that he might propose to you in such grand, top secret, auspicious circumstances."

My mouth dried. Percy had specifically requested of the Master of Mistlethwaite that he invite me? So that Percy could propose?

Oh, the shambles that had befallen that plan.

Andrew handed me the paper, carefully watching my face. "Having second thoughts?" he asked softly.

I shook my head. "No. I mean, I expected he'd propose soon—had wanted him to. I had no idea it would be this weekend. Indeed, I hadn't given his and my presence here together much thought after the first night when we discovered Lord Barclay's untimely demise." I looked up and met Andrew's gaze. "I care for him. But I have no desire to marry Percy Crofton. I desire to be Lady Harrigan. With all my heart."

A grin tipped the side of Andrew's lips, and he went back to his file while I read the missive Percy had penned.

My Dear Master of Mistlethwaite,

I am writing to you regarding the woman I wish to make my wife and would humbly ask your help. As I am certain you are aware, the Mistlethwaite games are legendary, and everyone longs for an invitation.

I wish to propose matrimony to Lady Emma Grace Hastings. You'll find she's just the sort of girl a peer of the realm would wish for in an English wife. I would beseech you, should you see fit to grant my request, that you invite the two of us to Mistlethwaite Manor for your secret games. I should enjoy if my proposal to this extraordinary young woman could be one of the most memorable events in her lifetime.

Your humble servant,

Percival Crofton, Lord Fairfax

My Dear Master of Mistlethwaite,

I am writing to you on behalf of the woman I wish to make my wife and would humbly ask your help. As I am certain you are aware, the Mistlethwaite games are legendary, and everyone longs for an invitation.

I wish to propose matrimony to Lady Emma Grace Hastings. You'll find she's just the sort of girl a peer of the realm would wish for in an English wife. I would beseech you, should you see fit to grant my request, that you invite the two of us to Mistlethwaite Manor for your secret games. I should enjoy if my proposal to this extraordinary young woman could be one of the most memorable events in her lifetime.

Your humble servant,

Percival Crofton,
Lord Fairfax

Poor Percy. I had no wish to break his heart, though I was gratified to know he thought so highly of me. Sadness on Percy's behalf pricked at my heart. It was regrettable. Until being confronted again with my first love, I'd thought myself on the way to a sort of love with Lord Fairfax. But it simply wasn't so.

And I'd determined that love was stronger than societal convention and my family's expectations. It was *my* life, and I wanted something more than to be the mistress of a grand estate. I wanted love. Genuine love.

I wanted it with Andrew Harrigan.

Rifling through a few more papers, I found another common sheet, topped with a bolded heading:

BERT HUMPHREY, LORD ASQUITH

The young Lord Asquith has recently inherited his title and estate upon his father's passing.

I have played at cards with him. Has a nasty penchant for gambling and obvious tells. Very arrogant, loves his drink. With only a modicum of liquor in him, he bet his entire estate against a bad hand.

He is utterly ruined.

It was nearly the easiest ruination I have ever conceived.

Such a child.

BERT HUMPHREY LORD ASQUITH

The young Lord Asquith has recently inherited his
title and estate upon his father's passing.

I have played at cards with him. Has a nasty penchant
for gambling and obvious tells. Very arrogant, loves
his drink. With only a modicum of liquor in him, he
bet his entire estate against a bad hand.

He is utterly ruined.

It was nearly the easiest ruination I have ever conceived.

Such a child.

"What a beast," I muttered, seething.

"Find something more?"

"Apparently Lord Barclay cheated Lord Asquith—whom he calls *a child*—out of his entire inheritance, ruining him utterly."

Andrew's mouth was a grim line. "I can relate to that a bit more than I care to."

"Oh, Andrew, I'm so sorry."

He shook his head. "It seemed Lord Barclay was a man of many underhanded talents. That cheating men parting them from their fortunes was all in a day's work for the miscreant."

"Oh, here is the poem. It's got a few lines scratched out, but I think this is where he did his final work. We might even be able to solve it with some of these added notes?"

I pulled a fresh sheet of paper, uncapped a bottle of ink, and dipped the quill. Quickly, I copied the poem, and then went back and put in the names I was certain of.

Two are staff, here to serve,
Our merriment to preserve. –Mr. and Mrs. Leonard

One of you has been bamboozled
One of you is worthless, utterly foozled

One born on the wrong side of the sheets –Mr. Campbell
Two of you, your spouses properly fleeced –Lord Villiers and
Lady Fulbright

For one of you, business has been bad –Mrs. Wentworth?
One of you, your innocence's been had –Lady Algernon

One of you is a commoner—just polite –William Angus
One of you a child, innocent not quite –Lord Asquith

One has been wronged, taken a long fall
Only one is the Master of it all. –Lord Barclay

Two are staff, here to serve,
Our merriment to preserve. —Mr. and Mrs. Leonard

One of you has been bamboozled
One of you is worthless, utterly foozled

One born on the wrong side of the sheets —Mr. Campbell
Two of you, your spouses properly fleeced —Lord Villers and
                                            Lady Fulbright

For one of you, business has been bad —Lady Wentworth
One of you, your innocence's been had —Lady Algernon

One of you is a commoner — just polite —William Angus
One of you a child, innocent not quite —Mr. Humphrey

One has been wronged, taken a long fall
Only one is the Master of it all. —Mr. Barclay

I handed the paper to Andrew. "I'm still not sure who was bamboozled, foozled, or took the long fall."

"Well, my father was certainly bamboozled by Horace Barclay when they did business together—but it wasn't directly me. And who are you? You don't seem to fit any of these remaining lines; I think we've got the right folks on the right lines. But all that's left is you, Percy, and me. Unless we *do* have someone wrong on the poem."

"Perhaps we'll run across something else. Let's keep looking," I said. Andrew nodded, putting my copied poem on the edge of the desk. My elbow knocked into a haphazardly stacked pile of papers, whooshing them to the ground.

"Bother," I muttered, standing to see where they'd all landed.

"Here, let me." Andrew bent to retrieve the fallen papers.

He gasped audibly.

"Andrew?"

"No." He breathed the word. His backside hit the floor hard.

"What is it?" I rounded the table, crouching in front of an entirely stunned Andrew. Carefully, I took the paper from his grasp. It was another plain sheet, but my blood chilled when I read the title:

PERCY CROFTON, LORD FAIRFAX

A most interesting, devious fellow. It seems he is behind the ruination of the Harrigan family, conveniently pinning all the underhanded doings on myself. Of course, I have done nothing to dissuade these rumors, as it only adds to my most notorious reputation.

Has requested help from the Master of Mistlethwaite to propose to Lady Hastings.

Given his own secrets, a most welcome addition to the party.

Should be worth thousands in blackmail.

Must be sure to note his shock when he realizes Horace Barclay and the Master of Mistlethwaite are one and the same.

PERCY CROFTON, LORD FAIRFAX

A most interesting, devious fellow. It seems he is behind the ruination of the Hattigan family, conveniently pinning all the underhanded doings on myself. Of course, I have done nothing to dissuade these rumors, as it only adds to my most notorious reputation.

Has requested help from the Master of Misslethwaite to propose to Lady Hastings. Given his own secrets, a most welcome addition to the party.

Should be worth thousands in blackmail.

Must be sure to note his shock when he realizes Horace Barclay and the Master of Misslethwaite are one and the same.

"Oh." Breath escaped in a rush and dizziness assaulted me. Dots spangled the edges of my vision as I tried to force my sluggish brain to work.

It was not Horace Barclay that had robbed Andrew of his family's fortune.

It had been Percival Crofton, Lord Fairfax, my nearly intended.

For a moment I thought I might retch.

I took several shaking breaths in through my mouth, trying to calm the tide of shock and detestation brewing inside.

"How could he have done this?" I whispered into the ether.

Andrew scrubbed his hands down his face. "I don't have words for this," he said.

I met his anguished gaze, unspoken words of shock, horror, and betrayal bouncing between us.

"Andrew, I don't know what to say." A part of me felt wildly guilty that the man I had planned to marry had done such a devious thing—to the man I was once engaged to, and now aimed to marry once again.

When had my life become so messy and entangled?

"There is nothing for you to say. But I will be saying plenty to Lord Fairfax"—he spat Percy's name— "when next we meet." A vein pulsed in Andrew's neck.

"Andrew, I'm so sorry. I swear, I had no idea."

He looked up, and his fierce expression melted upon seeing my obvious distress. He leaned forward, capturing my hands gently within his own. "Emma Grace, none of this is your fault. You could not have known, and even if you had, what could you have done to prevent it?"

"I could have refused him outright," I replied hotly.

A ghost of a smile hid at the corner of Andrew's lips. "And the vehemence is appreciated." He tipped forward, placing a quiet kiss on the end of my nose.

A crash reverberated through the ceiling of the hidden room. I flinched as Andrew jerked, both of us yanking our eyes upward.

Dust trickled down and unease gathered in my gut.

"I think it might be time to move. I don't know what that was, but now that we've gained a fuller picture of things, we need to find food and a place to hole up for the night. I'm not too keen on resting here with Lord Barclay's body," Andrew said as he shifted to his feet. Reaching down, he helped me to mine as well.

I shivered. "I have been in far more company with the dead these past two days than ever I desired." My stomach growled embarrassingly loudly. "But it seems I could use some food."

Andrew nodded. "Come. We'll do our best to sneak to the kitchens and then find someplace—maybe in the west wing, away from where we've been largely gathered. We need to wait things out. Our own staffs should be coming tomorrow to fetch us, and with the weather cleared, there should be little beyond the snow stopping them."

"Oh, Andrew, what if the snow drifts are too deep for the horses?" The sudden thought sent a new fissure of worry rocketing through my empty belly.

"Then we'll figure something else out." His jaw set and I knew he'd do everything in his power to find a way for us to escape this devilment of a manor. I shivered. My fingers were nearly numb, along with my toes. Cold prickled along my scalp and the back of my shoulders.

"Are you chilly?"

"Quite, I'm afraid."

"We'll go up to your chambers first and get you a wrap. No one has been stoking the fires. It may get colder yet in here before the dawn comes." Andrew drew me to him, rubbing his hands up and down my arms, creating a little warming friction and a lot of excitement in my stomach. Our society was not one that touched overmuch, and I found I craved Andrew's touch like a flower craved sunlight.

He stepped back and pulled the gun from his waistband once more. "Ready?"

"What do you think the others have been doing since we've been gone?" I whispered as I blew out the oil lamp, carefully picking it up and putting the tin of matches in my pocket. While we didn't want to risk more light being seen in the hidden hallways, it would be handy to have if we ended up in a darkened room again for the night. And I was sure we would. In a manor this large, surely there was some place safe enough from the other guests.

"I don't know, and I'm not sure I care to," Andrew whispered back. "We know for sure that at least one of them is a murderer. There can be no question that Lady Fulbright killed Lord Villiers. But I find it unlikely that she killed Mr. Leonard. It would be

difficult for a woman to achieve the needed strength." He glanced
back over his shoulder, face stricken. "I'm so sorry, Emma Grace.
Is this vein of conversation grieving?"

I shook my head. "Strangely not. While it's certainly not pleasant, I'm finding it somewhat therapeutic to recite the facts we do
know. Please continue."

He nodded, his voice a hush against the hidden walls. "I think
we can conclude that a man murdered Mr. Leonard. Was it Lord
Villiers in connection with Lady Fulbright?"

"I somehow doubt Lord Asquith committed the murders. He's
been inebriated almost the entire time we've been here." I was
careful to keep my weight on the front of my feet, so my heels made
as little noise as possible on the corridor floor.

"He did have motive if he wanted to conceal his foolishness in
gambling away his estate, but it does seem unlikely that he would
kill Leonard as well as Barclay."

We were nearing the stairs and we fell silent, taking them steadily
upward toward the third floor where our guest quarters were. We
reached the first of the rooms, illuminated by a little dot of light
against the far hallways of the hidden tunnel. Stopping to peer into
the room, I oriented myself. We were at the far end of the guest
hallway. I shivered, and not only due to the cold. Lady Algernon
had fallen to her death down the stairs just outside this room. It
was Lady Fulbright's room. A mattress in the room creaked and I
shifted my angle, peering through the hole like some Peeping Tom.
I cringed at my mental comparison, though it did not stop me from
gazing into the lit room.

Lady Fulbright sat on the edge of the bed, shaking like a leaf, staring into space. I realized it wasn't space so much that her eye was fixed upon, but at the spot on the corner of the nightstand where Lord Villiers's head had met its grisly end.

Why would she sit there? Was she in shock? The floor must still contain his blood stains. Whatever would cause her to sit there so entrenched in misery and wrapped in unholy memory? Maybe the whole debacle had driven her mad. Despite the grievances of her own making that plagued her, I pitied the woman.

Andrew gently pressed his fingers against my arm, urging me to move farther down the hallway. We passed Mrs. Wentworth's room, then Lord Villiers's, both dark and empty. A shard of light focused on the back wall, letting us know the gas lights were turned up in the next chamber. Andrew found the hole in the wall and peered in.

His entire body stiffened. My heart rate picked up, a cold sweat breaking out on the back of my neck and chilling me further. He glanced back at me, a sorrowful expression on his features. He nodded to the room then shook his head no.

I shook mine back. I needed to know what he saw. With reluctance, he pulled away from the peephole and let me move into his place.

My mouth dried, and my fingers shook.

Mr. Campbell's legs dangled in the air, a heavy chair a few paces away. Mr. Angus stared at him with dispassion, arms crossed over his chest, mouth set in a grim line as he tipped his head back to assess yet another dead man.

Perhaps his own handiwork.

CHAPTER TWENTY-THREE

I stared as stars spangled again in front of my vision. Could Mr. Angus be the killer? I blinked, trying to recall all memory of him from the weekend. He'd beaten me to the dining room. Would that have given him enough time to kill Lord Barclay first? My thoughts whirled. I flinched at the soft pressure of Andrew's arm around my shoulders, urging me to look away.

Tearing my eyes from the grisly scene in Mr. Campbell's chambers, I let Andrew lead me away. It took a little fumbling in the dark to find the hidden door to my own room as I hadn't left the gas lights on, but at last we found the lever. I quietly put the oil lamp and tin of matches on the ground. Just as I was about to lift it to allow us entrance into my chambers, the door creaked open. Light from the hallway illuminated a shadowy figure in the door.

Then the figure moved. In strode Percival Crofton. To my chambers. My eyes grew large, frozen on the lever. Andrew carefully pried my fingers from the metal, and we waited and watched. Andrew's fingers twined with mine, holding firmly, keeping me anchored.

Percy lit the gas mantle with a pop then scrutinized the room. Blood alternately boiled and chilled in my veins. This man had wronged Andrew and his family. He'd all but professed his love for me. Wanted to marry me. Had gone to such lengths as to petition the Master of Mistlethwaite Manor to aide him in his proposal. Had kissed my hand.

I wished I'd never set eyes on Percival Crofton. For several reasons.

Subconsciously I rubbed the back of my hand against my skirt.

His eyes were fevered, his actions jerky. "Where are you, Emma Grace?" he muttered.

Some of my fire dimmed at his words. Perhaps he was genuinely concerned for my safety. That did not excuse his vile actions toward the Harrigans, but on some strange level of my psyche, it was comforting to know he did care for my wellbeing. Perhaps Percy did have some connection to me.

All the same, my heart was where it should be now. With Andrew. I trained my eyes back to the room.

Percy scoured the room, lifting the pillows on the bed, rifling through my trunk. My face heated several shades of red when I

MURDER AT MISTLETHWAITE MANOR

realized my corset still sat, ties in a tangle, on a chair in the middle of the room. Percy saw it and stilled. He licked his lips. Hesitating a moment, he crossed to the chair, and reached an unsteady hand toward my undergarment.

He swallowed hard, his Adam's apple bobbing as he ran his finger over the rim of the intimate garment. My skin crawled. Beside me, Andrew was rigid, forearms taut, fist clenched around my fingers.

This was mortifying.

"This was supposed to be different, Emma Grace," Percy whispered to the empty room.

I grit my teeth.

Percy inhaled and glanced once more around the room. Growling, his hands fisted, and he set himself broodingly into one of the wingback chairs by the cold hearth.

"I swear I'll save you when I find you. I'll whisk you away from all this and fulfill your every desire. I'll atone for ever even desiring to come to cursed Mistlethwaite Manor." The words scraped from Percy's throat.

I bit the inside of my cheek. A day ago, my first impulse might have been to leap from my hiding spot behind the wall and comfort him. Percy was obviously distressed. But learning what he'd done to Andrew still festered like a coal under my skin, and I found myself wholly without the urge to go to him.

Andrew's stare burned into the side of my head, and I met his gaze in the dim illumination. Raw vulnerability scrolled across his features and my heart was moved fully to compassion. Brazenly, I crept closer, resting my cheek against his chest.

His hands came around my waist, hot against me, even through my layers of clothing. He inhaled silently and lost some of his rigidity.

A moment more and we looked again through the peep hole.

Percy still sat, fingers steepled in front of his face.

There was no hope of getting into my chambers to retrieve my wraps. At least not without detection by Percy. I was quite certain both of us wished to avoid a confrontation with Lord Fairfax, given the ominous circumstances.

Andrew jerked his head down the hallway.

Glancing down to make sure I wouldn't trip on my hem as we moved down the passageway, I held my breath.

A solitary rose petal rested on the threshold to my room.

My hand flew to my mouth as dread slithered through me, reminding me that we were likely not the only ones who knew of the passages' existence, and that we were far from safe.

CHAPTER
TWENTY-FOUR

I followed Andrew silently through a twist of turns until we found ourselves on the opposite side of the hallway and ensconced in his chamber.

Shivering, both with cold and a lingering ugsome trepidation, I rubbed my hands up and down my arms as Andrew opened his trunk, removing neatly folded articles of clothing until he pulled out a heavy cape.

"Here," he whispered, drawing the gloriously warm material snugly about my shoulders. It dusted the floor around my slighter frame, and it smelled deliciously of Andrew. The relief was nearly instant. My fingers and toes were still nearly numb, but the weight of the cape was like an added layer of security as well as some much-needed heat.

I could have stayed there, ensconced in Andrew's room with him, warm in his cape, relishing the gift of his presence. Relishing the fact that he still loved me.

"Better?" he mouthed.

I nodded. He returned the gesture then donned a heavier jacket himself.

We hesitated a moment, suddenly unsure of ourselves and each other.

My stomach took the initiative and gurgled loudly. Andrew smiled briefly and inclined his head toward the hidden tunnels again. apprehension, we stepped back into the darkness. I realized I'd left the oil lamp and matches in front of my chambers. It seemed less important now, given the risk of exposure with Percy still brooding in front of my fireplace. Andrew took the lead again, gun outstretched. Blessedly, we made it down to the lower level of the manor without further incident beyond a wrong turn.

Once we neared the labyrinth of tunnels by the library, we turned to the left, making our way to the other side of the manor to the kitchens. It was slow going as there were fewer lights and there were large gaps where we were left in the pitch dark. It was oddly comforting to be in the blackness. It made me feel invisible, and given the circumstances of the weekend, I longed to escape scrutiny—particularly as I did not know who I could or could not trust.

Andrew stopped abruptly.

"What is it?" I whispered near his ear.

He shivered and angled to face me, our chests touching in the tight confines of the secret tunnel. "There's nothing more. Only a door. The tunnel ends here." Uncertainty rang in his quiet words.

Anxiety slithered over my shoulders.

"I don't see anything through the peep hole. I think we're safe to cross the foyer."

"Is that where we are? The grand foyer?"

"Yes. We need to cross it, take the stairs, and find a way to the kitchens," Andrew said.

"There's a hidden panel in the far wall. I saw Mrs. Leonard appear from it when I first arrived—before she took me up to my room. I remember the general area where it is. If we can open it, we can disappear into the walls once more."

"Excellent plan, love."

Heat coiled all the way down to my frigid toes at Andrew's endearment.

"Stand back just a bit. This lever is jammed. I need both hands to crank it." He tucked the gun into the waistband of his pants, placed a brief kiss to my temple, then turned back to the door.

With a *crank,* the lever lifted, and we froze at the noise as it reverberated around us and into the echoing marble of the foyer. Gray light washed the grand room in a monochrome of shadows. Our search had wasted the night away and dawn must be nearing.

Taking a cautious step into the foyer, Andrew scanned our surroundings. He took another and breath left my lungs in a steady rhythm. We crept from the hidden tunnels into the room. The sun must have peeked over the horizon as the room flooded with early morning light while we crossed to the midpoint of the space. We were halfway to the stairs when every hair on my body stood on end.

"Stop!" Percy's strong voice echoed off the tiles of the grand entryway. "You vile Cretin!" he thundered at Andrew. "What have you done to her? What have you done to my *fiancé*? I'll see you hanged for this!" His eyes devoured the sight of me, draped in Andrew's cape.

"Percy, no," I started. Andrew shoved me behind him as we whirled to face the angry accusations.

"Lord Fairfax. I have done nothing for which I am ashamed. Though it would seem you, sir, have much to answer for. I've seen the evidence. I know it was you who ruined my family." Each word was a drop of hot lead, dripping to the floor, freezing in a spatter of jagged points.

Percy paled visibly in the dawn light winking over the edge of the earth. It flooded the foyer in bright morning sunshine that glittered like diamonds across the surface of the snow-covered world outside.

"You—you have no proof of these baseless accusations!" Percy shouted, though his tone was now strained. He shot a worried glance to my face, peeking out from behind Andrew's shoulder.

"To the contrary. I have a missive written in Horace Barclay's own hand regarding your duplicity. It seems we were both duped by the man—me into thinking he'd stolen the Harrigan fortunes, and you for having no idea the Mistlethwaite host was none other than the man you conveniently let take the blame for your misdeeds." Anger raged beneath the calm of Andrew's words. "Misdeeds I will see put to rights in a court of law."

"No. Emma Grace, come over here. Do not listen to this man's ramblings. He's clearly unhinged. You know I would never do such a thing. Come, let me take you away from this place of death!" Percy's jaw ticked.

"No, Percy," I said softly. "I'm sorry. It was never my intent to hurt you, but I fear my heart belongs to Andrew. I will stay with him." A weight lifted from my chest at my audible declaration.

Percy gripped his head, and for one dreadful moment, I feared he'd rip his face in two as anguish, and a slightly mad expression, rippled over him. Then a deadly calm took its place. Panic tickled my spine at the sudden transformation. I'd never witnessed this behavior in Percy before.

"No. No, I do not think that will be the case. Emma Grace, I have set my sights on you, and I *will* have you. Don't you know I ruined the blasted Harrigans so you'd see how easily they were manipulated? How easily they fell? Clearly, they could not care for you as I can. I, who masterminded their entire demise for your sake? I am much better suited to you."

My feet grew roots and my heart dropped like a stone.

"You are what I want. Did you know I even had you invited here, just so I could propose to you? I wrote to the Master of Mistlethwaite, begging him to help me make your engagement the talk of all England! *For you*!"

"Imagine your surprise to find it was Horace Barclay," Andrew said, edging us slowly toward the door. I stumbled, feet tangling in Andrew's over-long cape.

"You do not speak to me!" Percy roared, pulling a gun from his breast pocket, and aiming it at Andrew's heart.

Andrew froze, then carefully extended his arms to show that he was unarmed. But Mrs. Wentworth's gun was still tucked into the waistband at the back of his pants. Andrew's body shielded me from Percy's weapon, but the thought of anything happening to Andrew drove a wedge of fear straight through my chest.

"Percy, if you shoot me, you might hit Emma Grace. Let her leave the manor and then you can do whatever you like with me."

"No! I won't go!" A sob worked its way up my throat. Emotion, raw and potent, threatened to undo me.

A wicked grin twisted over Percy's lips. "Emma Grace, you come up here with me, and I'll let Harrigan go."

The wedge twisted cruelly in my heart.

"Emma Grace, don't do it," Andrew begged. "I don't trust that he won't harm you."

"Let Andrew go out the door first. Then I'll be in here with you," I countered. No way was I letting Andrew die if I could prevent it. While I absolutely didn't trust Percival Crofton anymore, I still didn't think he'd hurt me.

"I'm done playing games and countering moves. I've *killed* for you Emma Grace! Do you think I won't do it again? Least of all *him*? The very thing that stands in the way of my triumph?"

No.

"Percy, what have you done?" Tears pricked the back of my eyes as a dread so deep it nearly suffocated me took hold and squeezed my insides.

Percy's eyes took on a manic light. "I couldn't very well let Barclay live now, could I? He knew my secrets. He looked at me that first night, raised an eyebrow and had the gall to mock me with it. *I will not be mocked*! When everyone else had left, I doubled back and stabbed him with his own knife."

"But the blood—how did you hide what happened?" It was inconceivable he'd been able to kill Lord Barclay without getting a drop of blood on his person. Thoughts churned mercilessly in my brain, frantically putting pieces together, and desperately looking for a way out of this mess.

He'd come early enough to the dining room. He'd gotten stuck shutting the door that had blown open. Puzzle pieces clinked into place. I'd seen blood on the door handle. If Percy hadn't been shutting it, but opening it...

"You washed the blood off in the snow," I gasped the words.

"I knew you were quick, Emma Grace. Quite so. It wouldn't do for a man of my stature to have a dull wife. Yes. I scrubbed the blood from my hand off in the snow. Any other spatter was hidden against the black of my evening tails," he said smugly.

Bile rose in the back of my throat.

Andrew's fingers inched slowly toward the back of his waistband. I needed to keep Percy distracted.

I swallowed the bile back down and forced words to my lips. "The Leonards? Why them?"

"That dashed fool." Percy frowned. "I am sorry if he frightened you when he left the rose in your room. It was to be part of my grand gesture of our engagement. Though, I admit, it would have been far more romantic had I not had to kill the master of the games the night before. I acknowledge that was a mistake. A simple oversight. I wasn't sure how much Barclay had told the Leonards, and well, you know. Better safe than sorry."

Percy took one step nearer us. Andrew's hand inched back.

"And, and Mr., I mean, Lord Villiers?" I stammered.

"Oh, no. That wasn't me. That was truly all Lady Fulbright. Stroke of luck for me, wasn't it, that he enjoyed a bit of strangulation in his carnal pleasure."

Percy's eyes were so dilated, I could hardly see any blue around his enormous pupils. They were flat black. The color of sin. The color of death. The color of fear.

"Lady Algernon?" The words scraped claws of terror along the inside of my throat.

That smug smile flitted back onto his face. "I heard what she said while you were changing." His eyes widened further, and his tongue darted out to wet the rim of his lower lip. "I am most eager to see you in some of those garments lying about in your room, Emma Grace."

My stomach pitched and I nearly retched. Something akin to a growl sounded in Andrew's chest, reverberating through his back.

"But to answer your question, I *did* hear Lady Algernon speaking in your room. I heard it *all*. She said she saw the murderer. And well she might have. There was a noise as I was exiting from my"—he cleared his throat— "*business* with Mrs. Leonard. It might have been Lady Algernon, the fallen woman herself, doing who knows what, with who the devil knows, given her particular history. You know she was Campbell's mother? Hmmm. Quite so. We had such discussion once you flew from the library."

His eyes took on a manic light, his typical poise unraveling before my eyes.

"That really was bad form, Emma Grace, to leave so unexpectedly. You should have come to me. I'd have made sure you were all taken care of. See?" He waved his gun around, momentarily taking its aim from Andrew's heart. "See?" he repeated. "I even retrieved the gun I fired off in the library. I pitched it out the window, badly assuming I'd not need it again. But then you fled, and things...disintegrated. And here I find myself in need of it once more. But you needn't worry. I shall take care of everything. I am your protector. I am your husband. Your world will revolve around me." The self-assurance with which he said the words made my chest heave with unspoken indignation.

He was mad. Utterly mad!

"She's not yours just yet," Andrew said between clenched teeth. Percy's wolf-like gaze focused on Andrew like he'd forgotten he was there. Andrew's hand was halfway to the gun hidden in the back of his trousers.

"She has always been mine," Percy snapped. He took another step toward Andrew.

"What of Mr. Campbell? Did you kill him, too?" I asked, desperate to distract him from Andrew once more, to draw his attention so that Andrew could reach the gun that was surely our only hope of escape at this point. I hadn't come this far through this quagmire of a mess only to lose Andrew now.

"Mr. Campbell? How did you know..." Percy drifted off, his eyes narrowing at me. "I would have heard you come up the stairs. How did you find out about his death?"

"That doesn't matter right now," I said quickly. "Did—did you also do away with him? For my protection?" I added, stomach contorting painfully as I attempted to play his twisted game to gain us time.

Percy canted his head to the side, holding my gaze. "No. I did not kill Mr. Campbell. I believe it might have been that Angus fellow."

My heart lurched into the back of my throat, and I wanted to scream. I'd run out of bodies to talk about, and Percy was smiling at me now. As if I was the prey and he the all-powerful predator.

"Come to me, Emma Grace. We've no more secrets now, you and I. Let me dispose of this thing that dares to call himself a man, and we'll quit ourselves of this place. I'll sweep you to my estate at Heddon and make you the grand mistress of all my holdings. You shall be prized above all, and the envy of every woman in England."

Indecision warred within me. We needed another distraction. If I walked toward Percy, could I distract him enough that Andrew could gain access to his gun? Could I save Andrew in this way? Could I save us both by walking the tightrope of Percy's delusions?

"Percy, I—I," I stammered.

His brows drew together as anger clouded his black eyes. "Emma Grace, I tire of your dithering." There was a lethal edge to his voice that had every hair on my arms standing at attention.

Time stopped as three things suddenly happened at once. Percy lunged, gun outstretched, as Andrew simultaneously shoved me hard enough I tripped on the hem of his cape and crashed to the ground even as Andrew whipped his hand to the gun in his waistband.

My hip connected to the hard marble right as there was an explosion of fire, gunpowder, and a spray of blood that hazed red into the air.

Andrew shouted and smashed to the ground beside me, blood seeping from his shoulder. Percy howled and his gun clattered to the floor. Blood streamed from his hand. Wildly, I tore my horrified eyes from Andrew's bleeding arm and searched for his gun.

It was across the floor near the entrance to the far hallway.

Scrambling on all fours, I raced, hopped, and tripped toward the gun. Red dots danced at the edges of my vision, mocking me, telling me I'd never reach it in time. I didn't know if they were real or imaginary droplets of blood.

"Stop, Emma Grace." A gun cocked.

I froze, a whimper spilling from my lips as tears dripped, unbidden, down my cheeks. I turned, poised like a crab, staring in shock at the man I thought I'd known.

The man I would have married.

Horror and revulsion turned my stomach, and I couldn't keep the bile in anymore. I turned my head to the side as I emptied the meagre contents of my stomach onto the white and black titles.

Percy grimaced and paced back a step. Clutching his injured fingers to his chest, blood soaked into his shirt and suit jacket. "Emma Grace, come here," he commanded.

I shook my head, dizzy and crackling with terror.

"If you refuse me, you'll join his fate," Percy growled between clenched teeth. He pointed unsteadily toward Andrew.

"Run, Emma." Andrew grimaced, writhing in pain.

"What in the blue blazes is all the racket in here?"

My eyes shot up to find Lord Asquith swaying, thoroughly ossified, at the top of the stairs, drink in hand. He pitched forward, his drink spilling down from atop his perch and sloshing over Percy's arm and sprinkling alcohol onto his injury.

"Tarnation, you clodpate!" Percy hollered, bleeding hand clutched tighter to his chest.

I took the opportunity to make a dive for the gun but was brought up short as a hand reached down, beat me to it, and picked up the gun.

I stared up into the eyes of William Angus.

I was trapped between two murderers.

Chapter
Twenty-Five

"Run," Mr. Angus whispered. He gripped the gun and raised it level with Percy's chest. I scrambled, slipping to my feet.

"Emma Grace, don't you leave me. Come here to my side, and I won't let this blackguard touch you." Percy had his weapon trained on William Angus. And for the moment, I realized I stood between the two men, between their two firearms, and between life and death.

It was time to take my fate into my own hands.

"Lady Hastings, if you'd care to just step behind me," Mr. Angus said, his eyes and his gun never wavering from Percival Crofton.

"Go, Emma," Andrew grunted.

Torn between racing to the man I loved and removing myself from harm's way, my gaze fixed on Andrew.

He nodded at me, pained, but confident. Stifling a whimper, I shuffled until I was behind Mr. Angus and sheltered by the wall of the corridor and his body. I couldn't make myself move any farther from Andrew.

I watched on in horror, helpless to do anything else.

"This is done then, Emma Grace. You've made your decision." Percy's face shuttered, a stony, terrible determination crawling over his face. "There will be no more forgiveness. You'll share your lover's fate." He sneered and pointed the gun back at Andrew who had crept along the floor, nearer to Percy. A bloody smear sullied the tiles behind him. I bit the inside of my cheek to keep from crying out.

What was Andrew doing?

"Lord Fairfax, you are under arrest for the murders of Horace Barclay, Leo and Agnes Leonard, and Rose Algernon." Mr. Angus's voice rang clearly.

"Under arrest?" Percy snorted. "By whom? You? You pathetic little man. To think you have any power over me is laughable."

"I'm Detective Chief Inspector Jeffery Dyer of Scotland Yard. I came here under false pretenses. Thanks to some anonymous tips—probably former guests—we've had our eyes on Horace Barclay's underhanded doings for months. Though I must confess, this is certainly a wilder ride and more corruption than I expected to find."

Percy gaped. In truth, my own mouth might have been hanging open as well.

"I'm a peer of the realm. I, I'm a lord! You have no authority over me!" Percy sputtered.

"I may be a commoner, sir," Mr. Angus—Detective Chief Inspector Dyer—said icily, "but I assure you I have the full force of the law on my side." He smiled without mirth. "Not even Prince Edward is beyond the arm of the law, as I'm sure you remember his appearances in court four years ago."

"Or I could just shoot you now," Percy said, fury etched into his face.

I screamed as Percy whipped his arm back toward the inspector. Lord Asquith, who I'd completely forgotten about until that moment, threw his empty glass at Percy from where he still stood atop the staircase.

The glass smashed into the back of Percy's head. His shot went wild, chipping plaster down from the ceiling, and consequently, causing the inspector's shot to miss as well, embedding into the door of the closet where we'd found Mr. Leonard's corpse.

Andrew kicked out solidly, catching Percy in the back of the knees, and he crumpled.

Quicker than butter melting on hot toast, Inspector Dyer raced to Percy's side, flipped him over onto his gut, and dug out a pair of Twister manacles. Wrapping the chain securely around Percy's wrists and fitting the T-shaped metal rods together, Percy, at last, lay stunned and restrained.

Sobs breaking from my throat, I rushed to Andrew's side.

"Andrew," I gasped. "What do I do?" I looked helplessly at his bleeding shoulder.

"I'm all right now," he insisted. His face was white as clotted cream and his lips were gray.

"Put pressure on the bleeding on both sides, Miss," Inspector Dyer instructed.

"Yes, yes, of course," I muttered, ripping off Andrew's cape I still wore, and pressing the material over his wounds.

Andrew groaned, his eyes fluttering shut.

"Andrew Harrigan, don't you dare lose consciousness!" I commanded.

"Lord Asquith, are you too inebriated to fetch some linen sheets or bandages, whichever you can find first?"

"I assure you; this spectacle has knocked the drink right out of me." The young man mopped his brow and turned to go in search of the required materials.

"Bring back some brandy if you haven't drunk it all!" the inspector hollered after him.

"Andrew, what can I do?" I asked again.

He smiled weakly. "Just be here with me."

"I'll never leave you again." One of my tears dripped onto his cheek but I didn't dare move my hands from his wound to wipe it away.

"Promise?" he asked.

"Promise."

He frowned. "You're not hurt, are you? I see,"—he swallowed painfully— "you've got blood on you."

I glanced down. "It's not mine. I think it's yours."

"Oh. All right. So long as it doesn't belong to you."

"But it does. Because it's yours."

He smiled, gray lips stretching wide. He raised his hand to my cheek, and I clasped it there. His skin was cold, but his pulse moved, and for that I was extremely grateful.

Percy howled in fury, face mottled, spittle flying as he raged insults at the lot of us. Inspector Dyer hauled him to his feet. Struggling with Percy's fit, muscled body, the inspector twisted the chains of the manacles and Percy howled louder, pain lacing the notes.

"Shove it now, or I'll twist it snug enough I'll snap your wrist bones. Do I make myself clear?" Inspector Dyer's voice was calm and tight, a coiled spring ready to fly.

Percy quieted, though he still glared in murderous wrath.

Somewhere a clock chimed eight bells.

"Oh, surely someone's servant will arrive soon. Tell me this is nearly over, Andrew," I said, smoothing the hair off his brow.

"I found a fresh tablecloth! Will that work?" Lord Asquith appeared at the top of the stairs again, waving a pale-yellow folded cloth. I glanced at the inspector. I knew nothing of these sorts of ministrations. Training to be lady of the manor hadn't exactly prepared me for gunshot wounds in the middle of the grand foyer.

"Aye. Bring them down," Inspector Dyer said.

Lord Asquith trotted down the stairs, bottle of spirits and table-cloth in hand.

"Here." He thrust them at me.

"Um," I hummed.

The inspector rolled his eyes and I bristled, despite the circumstances. "Right. Asquith, go fetch some rope or some silk cording from some of the drapes. And bring me a chair from the dining room." He turned to me as Lord Asquith heaved a sigh and trudged back up the stairs. "Here's what you need to do, Lady Hastings."

With instructions from Inspector Dyer and a few mishaps on my part, we finally staunched the worst of the bleeding. I fashioned the remains of the once-pristine tablecloth into a makeshift sling. Fortunately, the bullet seemed to have gone clear through.

"Slide it just over my shoulder there. That's it," Andrew encouraged weakly. He was leaned up against the wall, chilly, but comfortable enough. Neither of us relished the idea of being in the same room as Percy Crofton, but neither did we want him out of our sights either.

"I've got all the cording from the draperies in the salon. Will these be enough?" Lord Asquith held up his mass of green silk drapery cords like a golden trophy.

"Bring them down and fetch us the chair. We'll tie this blackguard up and perhaps have a pot of tea," Inspector Dyer said, a jovial note to his tone.

I had to admit, a pot of steaming tea did sound divine.

Lord Asquith made short work of bringing in a chair, and then the two men hoisted Percy into it and tied him fast, arms still secured in the manacles.

"All this time, you've, you've been from the police?" I asked as the inspector tied off the last green knot.

"I have. It's been carriwitchett trying to get solid details about Barclay. Knowing what I do now, I assume everyone was afraid of the man's blackmail. No wonder no one ever spoke up. We had an anonymous tip off on Barclay's movements that led us to think Barclay might be attending the Mistlethwaite Christmas festivities. Mr. Angus is known to us, and when he received an invitation, I took Mr. Angus's spot as I'm a close likeness of the man, and well I did. Look at the mess things have turned out. I was as surprised as everybody else when Lord Barclay turned out to be our host." He shrugged. "While I can't say I'm thrilled to report half the guests murdered by none other than one of the most influential peers of the realm, I suspect my superiors will be pleased that Barclay's tyranny is at an end, and that a dangerous criminal has been apprehended." He shot Percy a dirty glare. Percy snarled at the man.

"Prove it," Percy growled.

"I shall. You, realizing who Barclay was, doubled back and stabbed him with the knife you found on Barclay's desk. I noted it in the room when we first gathered. Fearing the Leonards knew your secrets as well, you first bashed in Mr. Leonard's head with a board underneath the stairwell. Upon removing the husband, you strangled Mrs. Leonard in the library with what you found on hand, not realizing it was Lady Hasting's evening wrap. I suspected you of Lady Algernon's demise. You were the one standing closest to her, and she'd just confessed to you that she knew who the murderer was. You simply had to off her. Let us not forget that I heard your confession moments ago. I shall testify with all haste against you."

Percy turned his face away, refusing to look at the man.

"I, for one, am grateful for your assistance, particularly there at the end," Andrew said with a half-smile.

The inspector nodded.

"You saved my life," I added.

"I confess, I had my early suspicions that possibly the young lady and that jackanapes were in the thick of things. Then I suspected the two of you were in cahoots," Inspector Dyer said with a wry grin. "Had I realized just how innocent the two of you were, I'd have revealed myself to you earlier."

"That's it. The poem," Andrew said excitedly. "Emma Grace, you were the bamboozled one. Percy was the foozled one—Barclay double crossed his intentions—and I was the one that was wronged. By Percy. We did it. We solved the dastardly poem." Andrew nodded in satisfaction.

"Did you then? Did you figure out each line?" Inspector Dyer asked.

"Emma Grace, do you still have the paper you wrote the poem on?" Andrew asked.

"I do." I pulled out the wrinkled paper from my pocket and smoothed it out. I read it out.

"Two are staff, here to serve, our merriment to preserve. That's Mr. and Mrs. Leonard. One of you has been bamboozled—me," I said, relieved it wasn't my innocence in question anymore. "Percy fooled me completely in regard to his character." I didn't look at him. Andrew squeezed my hand.

"One of you is worthless, utterly foozled. Percy." My eyes flew to the horrible man. He glared at me. "He had no idea his original misdeed would be the cause of Lord Barclay's double crossing." Percy snarled again, teeth shining.

"One born on the wrong side of the sheets. Poor Mr. Campbell." I turned to the inspector. "Andrew and I found Lord Barclay's secret study. We found evidence that Lord Barclay and Lady Algernon had an affair when she was quite young—and that it resulted in Mr. Campbell. Wait—we saw you with his hanged body!"

"I only found him. He hanged himself. I can only assume it was his way of dealing with the stress of the murders and maybe the shock of discovering his parentage? Stood on a chair then knocked it from under his own feet. I heard the thump and came to investigate, but he was gone by the time I got there. You found a secret study?" Inspector Dyer's eyebrows drew up his forehead.

"We did. And Lord Barclay's body. We think he came to after the initial attempt on his life, moved himself, then bled out in the hallway. I'll show you once he's properly dealt with." Andrew nodded to Percy. Percy put his nose in the air and turned his face from Andrew, refusing even to acknowledge his presence. "Go on, Emma Grace. Finish it out," Andrew encouraged.

I nodded. "Two of you, your spouses properly fleeced—clearly this was Lord Villiers and Lady Fulbright. Oh, where is Lady Fulbright? And Mrs. Wentworth?"

"Last I saw, Lady Fulbright locked herself in her chambers. I fear the stress of things may have driven her mad," the inspector said with regret. "As to Mrs. Wentworth, I haven't seen her, but I doubt she's a threat to anyone beyond a sound tongue lashing. Vile woman."

I nodded. Heaviness for Lady Fulbright settled in my chest. Mrs. Wentworth would be found at some point, but with Percy caught, neither lady was in immediate danger. I cleared my throat. "For one of you, business has been bad. That is Mrs. Wentworth. I remember hearing about it—her husband was in the wool trade. I think Lord Barclay struck an underhanded deal with Mr. Wentworth. He—he shot himself, and Mrs. Wentworth blamed Lord Barclay. One of you, your innocence's been had. Lady Algernon, as we agreed," I rushed on quickly, heat still flushing my cheeks over the implications of that line of the poem. "One of you is a commoner—just polite." My eyes flew to the inspector. He nodded. "Well, I guess this is you, sir, though you're not William Angus."

"I am not, but for the purposes of the poem, we'll say I am."

"One of you a child, innocent not quite. Lord Asquith, I believe this line describes you."

"I'm certain it does." The young man dragged a hand down his face. He seemed to have aged decades over the weekend.

"The last lines are, One has been wronged, taken a long fall." I glanced at Andrew. "This is your family."

He nodded, squeezing my hand with his uninjured one.

"And then, only one is the Master of it all—which, I'd have said was Lord Barclay starting out, but now that we're at the end of things, I think this might be Andrew, too," I said looking at him again. "Because he's the one that finally figured out all the clues."

"A job well done," Inspector Dyer confirmed.

A jingling of bells sounded from down the lane.

"Oh, they've come at last!" I murmured.

"Help me up, Emma Grace," Andrew said, his thumb rubbing soft strokes over the back of mine.

I helped him to his feet, and together, we stood shivering at the window and watched.

Outside, the sunlight sparkled on the fresh snow, white and pristine as far as the eye could see. A sleigh pulled by four horses, snow bouncing up to their knees tromped down the long entryway up to Mistlethwaite Manor. As they drew nearer, my heart rejoiced, recognizing my family's own sleigh and our trusted footman.

Help was at hand! The nightmare was finally over.

I'd never been so happy to leave a party as I was to make myself scarce from Mistlethwaite Manor.

CHAPTER
TWENTY-SIX

A wash of spring air drifted through the open window,
rustling the draperies of the living room.

Christmas, murder, and Mistlethwaite Manor were a distant
dream. Occasionally a nightmare still visited in the dark of night
from which I'd awake, slaked in sweat, fear raw in the back of my
mouth. But it was done.

And today, Andrew—who'd written to say his shoulder had
healed—was coming to speak to Father. Though Father had been
greatly distraught at hearing what had befallen me at Mistlethwaite, he was still leery of letting me marry into the Harrigan
family. Not because he thought any less of Andrew. Indeed, Father

thought he was a good man, and more so after the high praise of the inspector and police for his bravery. But he worried how he would provide for me and any children we might have.

I felt as if I stood on the edge of a precipice. By this evening, I'd either have Andrew's ring on my finger, or I'd be packing my bags for Gretna Green. Because I had resolved to marry Andrew. My heart was his, and I wanted a future with him, regardless of what may come. Love was worth that. Andrew was worth that.

A soft knock sounded at the door, and I frowned. It was too early for Andrew's appearance. He wasn't coming for yet another hour.

"Miss, a Mr. Kylverson is here to see you. Says he's a barrister from London." A maid dipped a curtsy as she relayed the message.

"And he says he's here to see *me*?" I asked, rising from the couch where I'd been attempting to read a book.

"He does, Miss."

"Well, send him in then."

A moment later, an older gentleman shuffled in, a briefcase in his hand. The maid that had shown him in stood just inside the open door, a dutiful chaperone.

The older gentleman addressed me. "The young Lady Hastings, I presume?"

"Yes. May I enquire as to what this is about?"

"Of course, but let us sit. I am Mr. Matthew Kylverson, Esquire. I represented Horace Barclay's interests."

I recoiled at the name.

"Forgive me. I didn't intend to stir up unwanted memories. I'll be brief. As things have settled and his affairs have been put in order, it would seem that you are the recipient of the ten thousand pound prize as you were the one to figure out all of Lord Barclay's clues to his Christmas puzzle."

I gaped like a fish on dry land. "I beg your pardon?" I finally gasped.

He repeated himself.

"How, how can that be?" I said in wonderment.

"It is clearly stated in his will that the winner of his Christmas riddle was to inherit the promised ten thousand pounds. Additionally, as he has now passed, as has his issue—"

"Mr. Campbell, you mean?" I interrupted rudely.

"Yes. Mr. Campbell was listed as Lord Barclay's beneficiary. But as both men have passed away, through the strange twist of events that took place in December, and as the only other inheritor listed in Lord Barclay's will, you are also the inheritor of Mistlethwaite Manor and the rest of Lord Barclay's assets."

I sat in utter stupefaction.

"You did solve the riddle, did you not? We ascertained from Lord Asquith that you were the one who solved it." Mr. Kylverson raised a bushy gray eyebrow.

My head was spinning but snagged on one thought. "If, if I was not the one who solved the riddle, would all the money and the manor go to that person instead?"

Mr. Kylverson frowned a bit, thinking. "It would be unorthodox, and we'd need to corroborate your story with Detective Chief

Inspector Dyer, but yes, all the money and manor would go to the person who solved the riddle."

A smile stole over my face as I glimpsed Andrew's strong form in the distance, riding confidently in his saddle up the lane toward my house.

"It was Andrew Harrigan that solved the riddle. The money and the manor should rightfully go to him."

EPILOGUE

A crisp breeze rustled the gossamer trailing around the pillars set up along the garden path as my slippered feet softly crunched the fresh gravel that had been laid especially for my wedding.

My father walked proudly beside me, my arm tucked into the crook of his elbow. He patted my hand. "I'm very proud of you, Emma Grace," he whispered.

I smiled behind my veil, but before I could respond, we rounded the bend and stood ready to walk to the makeshift altar where the minister awaited, and where Andrew stood, resplendent in his suit, waiting for me.

Father escorted me to the front and a collective sigh rose up from those gathered to witness our marriage. With a slight tremor in his hands, Father clasped my fingers, raised my veil, and kissed my cheek, then transferred my hands to Andrew's.

Andrew's grip was solid, though he swallowed hard, and his eyes searched my face. I loved him so. I squeezed his hands lightly and a silly grin broke out on his face.

It was an intimate ceremony, much to my mother's social dismay. Only our friends—the ones who had not forsaken Andrew when he'd lost his fortune, and none of those who had flocked to him once more when it had been made public that he'd become the inheritor of the vast Mistlethwaite estate—were in attendance. Those we loved, and those who loved us. And a certain Detective Chief Inspector who was smiling widely from the second row.

When the time came for Andrew to kiss me, we hesitated just a moment, a thousand unsaid words and feelings passing between us.

The world fell away as his thumb gently traced my chin. "From my life's greatest tragedy has come my life's greatest gift."

And then he kissed me.

THANKS

There are so many unseen forces that go into the making of a story, and even more yet that go into the making of a book. I'm certain to forget someone here, and for any lapses, I do apologize.

So many thanks to Amanda. Your encouragement during the writing of Mistlethwaite was invaluable. Your excitement for the characters and the intrigue kept me writing and kept me pushing through. Your friendship has been one of those glorious good gifts!

Ashley—thank you for reading the super rough copy of this and endorsing it anyway.

Ava, your enthusiasm was catching!

Mom, as always, I so appreciate your willingness to drop everything to help me.

Denica, your suggestions were invaluable.

Brittany, you astound me. You are a delightful human in every possible way, and each day, I am grateful for your friendship, your insight, and your generosity.

Emilie—you wizard of creativity! This cover is my very favorite of all my books to date!

Thank you to the Quill & Flame folks—ya'll are the BEST team. Many thanks for all the "fluffing."

Husband, thank you for the time to write. A story isn't much good without time to write it.

To my children—your zest for life, and delight for my books, characters, and plots is so wonderful. I love that you are starting to make your own stories and illustrations. I hope you never lose the joy you exhibit as you freely create your own imaginary worlds.

To all of you who are reading this, bless you for sticking it out this long and reading the acknowledgments anyway. I am first and foremost a trauma writer, and *Mistlethwaite* popped into my head nearly fully fleshed during a particularly stressful Christmas season. I'm so grateful for a constructive outlet for the crazy, and hope you've enjoyed the ride as well. I'd love to hear from you—thoughts, comments, questions, snide remarks. I enjoy them all.

If you'd like to reach out to me, please feel free. I respond to every email I receive. You can drop me a line at aj@ajskelly.com or find me at @a.j.skelly on Instagram, or Readers of AJ Skelly on Facebook (I really need a catchier name for the group...). If you'd like to ensure you don't miss any new book news, giveaways, or random AJ factoids, you can subscribe to my newsletter through my website: www.ajskelly.com.

Blessings and Christmas joy all the year round. Perhaps without the murder and mayhem. Unless it's in a book.

Cheers!

-AJ

IF YOU LIKED

CONSIDER CHECKING OUT MORE QUILL & FLAME PUBLISHING HOUSE TITLES

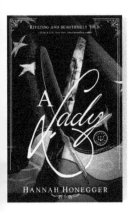

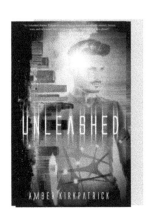

HEAT WITHOUT THE SCORCH

Quill & Flame
PUBLISHING HOUSE

www.quillandflame.com